When Love Was
Clean Underwear

When Love Was
Clean Underwear

Susan Barr-Toman

Many Voices Project Winner

First Edition
Library of Congress Control Number: 2008934507
ISBN: 978-0-89823-243-1
MVP Number 117
Cover and interior book design/photograph by Alex Ehlen
Author photograph by Sarah Barr

The publication of *When Love Was Clean Underwear* is made possible by the generous support of the Jerome Foundation and other contributors to New Rivers Press.

For academic permission please contact Frederick T. Courtright at 570-839-7477 or permdude@eclipse.net. For all other permissions, contact The Copyright Clearance Center at 978-750-8400 or info@copyright.com.

New Rivers Press is a nonprofit literary press associated with
Minnesota State University Moorhead.

Wayne Gudmundson, Director
Alan Davis, Senior Editor
Donna Carlson, Managing Editor
Allen Sheets, Art Director
Thom Tammaro, Poetry Editor
Kevin Carollo, MVP Poetry Coordinator
Liz Severn, MVP Fiction Coordinator
Frances Zimmerman, Business Manager
    Publishing Interns: Samantha Jones, Andrew Olson
    When Love Was Clean Underwear Book Team: Mary Huyck Mulka, Amber Olds,
        Jessica Riepe, Andrea Vasquez
    Editorial Interns: Michael Beeman, Mary Huyck Mulka, Nathan Logan,
        Kayla Lundgren, Tarver Mathison, Amber Olds,
        Jessica Riepe, Alyssa Schafer, Andrea Vasquez
    Design Interns: Alex Ehlen, Andrew Kerr, Erin Malkowski,
        Megan McCleary, Lindsay Stokes

Printed in the United States of America.

New Rivers Press
c/o MSUM
1104 7th Avenue South
Moorhead, MN 56563
www.newriverspress.com

To Ian and Oona

Chapter One

Lucy took the oxygen tubes out of her mother's nose and turned off the tank so they could share a last cigarette together. Marge's last cigarette. It was October 30, Mischief Night, the day her mother Marge had chosen in the hope of being buried on All Souls' Day. She chose the time, around eleven fifteen p.m., so that she could watch the lead story on the eleven o'clock news; she no longer cared to hear the five-day forecast.

They sat in the dining room, which had been converted into a makeshift hospital room with an adjustable bed, a commode, a TV tray covered with prescription bottles, and the oxygen tanks. Lucy held the brown cigarette to her mother's mouth. The smoke hung about Marge's face. Her lungs could barely pull it in or force it out, but she still enjoyed the smell and taste.

The lead news story had proven a disappointment. The "Werewolf Boy" from South America had plastic surgery at Children's Hospital to remove the thick hair covering one side of his face; skin grafts were required. Instead of after-pictures of the boy's face following the procedure, they aired pre-surgery video. Dr. Eugene McCormick, a man in his early fifties wearing wire-rimmed glasses and a white medical jacket, outlined an area of the boy's face with a black marker, while the anchorwoman stated that the boy was recuperating and in stable condition.

"He is the same," Marge said through parched lips, as she turned her face away.

She had motioned to Lucy that it was time. Reluctantly, Lucy let go of the aluminum-foil-covered antenna of their old television. She didn't want to kill her mother. She didn't know whether she *could* kill her mother.

Lucy took a drag and then offered the cigarette to her mother again. Closing her eyes, Marge parted her lips and sucked ever so slightly on the filter. She opened her mouth to let the last of the smoke escape, and studied its rise.

Then Lucy tapped out the cigarette in the ashtray until every ember was extinguished. She went into the kitchen to empty and wash the ashtray, a ritual Marge insisted upon after each cigarette. One that Lucy was grateful for now; it gave her just a few more minutes. "Smoking doesn't have to be a dirty habit," Marge would say.

As Lucy returned to the dining room, Marge pointed to her purse. Lucy knew what she wanted — the index cards with Marge's final to-do list. Each step of Marge's death was printed clearly, ingrained in blue ink, on its own index card. In the past few weeks, she'd meticulously jotted down notes while watching reruns of *Columbo* and other detective shows. From these notes, she created the concise, detailed to-do list. For as long as Lucy could remember, index cards were how Marge ordered the days, weeks, and seasons of her life. She kept all but these final ones in a recipe box on the kitchen windowsill. Mostly they were instructions on keeping house, some recipes — Marge's parting gift to Lucy "so she wouldn't have to reinvent the wheel every morning."

Protest was futile. Lucy cautiously brought up that some in the Church might consider it a mortal sin. Marge said, "I've got that covered." Lucy pleaded that she wasn't up to the task, maybe there was someone else, perhaps Marge could do it on her own?

"I gave birth to you. This is the least you could do for your poor dying mother," Marge replied. The conversations ended always with Marge's standard end-of-discussion scowl.

Lucy sat next to her mother, and when Marge nodded, Lucy read from the first card:

Number One: Place pillow over my face and apply firm but gentle pressure for a minimum of five minutes.

Marge reached for the pillow behind her head. Lucy took it with one hand and looked for a place to set the stack of index cards. Finally, she decided to put them on Marge's lap, then she stood. She wanted to say something or do something meaningful but Marge seemed eager to get on with it. Afraid she'd fail her mother, Lucy started, "Mom . . . "

Marge calmly waved her off and motioned for the pillow. Lucy took a deep swallow, put the pillow over Marge's face, bending its ends around her head, and held it tight. Her mother's body became rigid. Her fists pushed into the mattress. Marge had warned Lucy not to break her nose. People would suspect foul play. And she didn't want black eyes for her funeral. "It's not that I'm vain," she'd said, "I just want to be presentable."

After a few moments, Lucy's hands were wet with perspiration; her joints ached from the pressure, the tension. Her mother lay still. Lucy had forgotten to check the time before starting. How did she get stuck doing this? Who else would do it? Her father was dead. Her sister Anne would never have agreed to this, and Marge would never have asked her.

Lucy lifted the pillow.

"Mom, are you there?"

Marge's eyes opened, startling Lucy, then Marge began coughing.

"Are you okay?" asked Lucy.

Her mother moved her head. Lucy couldn't decipher if she was shaking it or nodding.

"Do you want a glass of water?"

Marge's coughing subsided and she glared at Lucy.

"Get the egg timer," she whispered with what was left of her voice.

When Lucy returned, Marge set the timer for five minutes. Pushing aside prescription bottles, she positioned it on the TV tray next to her. Then, she pressed the button to recline the bed. She motioned for Lucy to place the pillow over her head again.

"I'm not sure I want to do this!" Lucy started crying. Marge patted her daughter's shoulder and reset the timer. She pushed the pillow to Lucy.

"Okay, okay," Lucy mouthed. Right before she put the pillow over her mother's face for the second time, she noticed Marge blowing air out of her mouth. Her hands lay across her chest, her gnarled fingers neatly intertwined and pressing down. Death could not come fast enough for Marge.

Her mother had been ready for death since her husband Joseph died twelve years ago. She'd curled into herself like a pill bug, only her armor left showing. Marge never forgave Joseph for dying so unexpectedly, so poetically, and so well before her. His dying was not in the plan. He'd broken their agreement. He'd abandoned her.

Joseph Pescitelli was a house framer. One day on the job, he stopped hammering, clutched his chest, and slid down a wood stud until his tool belt clunked against the plywood floor. It was all one fluid motion. He died with one hand on his chest and the other still holding his hammer.

Theirs had been a May-December romance. Joseph was twenty-two years older and a confirmed bachelor when he met Marge. But he had always acted younger than his age and she older. It was as if, in marrying Joseph despite her family's disapproval, Marge O'Connell had committed her one act of youthful passion and been done with it. At the young age of fifty, Marge seemed to welcome the cancer, having grown bored and frustrated with living. She was furious that she was confined to a hospital bed with oxygen tubes up her nose, peeing in a pot in the middle of the very same dining room in which she conducted Christmas and Easter celebrations for thirty-some years. Her dying was neither poetic nor quick.

The egg timer ticked the seconds. Lucy stared at the white pillow covering her mother's face until she saw spots. Then she looked to the window and saw the reflection of the simple circular chandelier, hovering in the darkness. A lone white feather that must have escaped the pillow slowly swayed back and forth making its way to the bed until Lucy blew it away. Marge's body was tense and shook slightly. Lucy stood, her arms straight, pushing down. Her elbows and knuckles ached. The dark hair on her arms stood on edge in contrast to the brightness of the room. Everything seemed alive and watchful. The egg timer, the feather, the chandelier — all witnesses. Lucy turned her face away and stared at the twisted zigzag lines of the television screen. Her vision was already blurred with tears as she tried not to notice her mother's feet twitching under the blankets like two land-bound fish. Voices from another channel cut in and out. She couldn't make out what they were selling. The health reporter spoke with great earnestness about the merits of drinking tea. The elderly British people she interviewed proclaimed that their religious consumption of tea was the reason for their longevity. Many had grandparents who had lived well into their nineties. The Pescitellis were coffee drinkers. Marge's body jolted, once, twice, three times. Lucy held tight onto the pillow letting her tears fall from her jaw. Her throat ached, trying to release a cry. She swallowed. Next up on the news was a man who had invented a device for yanking trapped plastic bags from tree limbs. The news took a break to advertise the following day's six o'clock news. The egg timer buzzed, rattling against the metal TV tray.

Lucy lifted the pillow and held it against her chest. Marge's milky blue eyes were open. Lucy hadn't expected that. She waved her hand in front of them; they didn't blink.

"Mom? Mom? Are you there?"

Nothing.

"Are you dead, Mom?"

Number Two: Make absolutely sure I am dead.

Lucy lay her head on her mother's chest. Sometimes when she was little, Lucy woke up to the sound of her father snoring in the front bedroom and the noise of the television downstairs. There, her mother had fallen asleep in her recliner, the flickering light on her still body. Quietly, Lucy climbed onto her lap and listened to her mother's heart beating, her soft murmuring in her sleep. Now there was no sound, no motion.

As instructed, Lucy placed a hand-held mirror in front of Marge's nose and mouth. It didn't fog up. She couldn't make the call to the doctor unless she was absolutely sure Marge was dead; her mother had emphasized that several times. Lucy checked her mother's wrist for a pulse.

"Mom? Are you there?" Lucy stood above her and gently shook her shoulders. Marge's body was limp. Lucy placed Marge's hands on her chest as they did at the funeral home where she worked. Her mother's hands were rough. The perpetual cycle of scrubbing, washing, and scouring had left her hands with the swollen, bruised look of a fisherman's face after decades of exposure to salt air.

Number Three: Place pillow under my head.

After closely inspecting the pillow for any traces of bodily fluid, Lucy returned it to its place under Marge's head. She straightened Marge's faded gray-streaked strawberry blond hair. While the muscles in Marge's face were relaxed, Lucy could still see the line between her eyes. Oddly, in death Marge appeared younger. For a moment Lucy considered holding her in her arms, but her mother's eyes were still watching. Instead, she quickly kissed her forehead, something she would never have done while her mother was alive. In her mother's house, love was clean underwear, not hugs and kisses. When she stroked Marge's cheek, she was surprised by its softness and the light peach fuzz. She assumed her skin would feel more like burlap than silk. Her sister Anne bore a very strong resemblance to Marge — tall, slender, and fair with freckled skin and thin lips. Lucy took after her father, which meant she was shorter, rounder, her skin olive. Her dark hair was noticeable on her upper lip and sideburns, more pronounced on her arms and legs than the average woman's. Lucy couldn't help but wonder if Marge's interest in the Werewolf Boy was an indirect slight at her.

Number Four: Reinsert oxygen tubes.

Lucy released a heavy sigh, not realizing she'd been holding her breath. The tubing rested on Marge's throat. Lucy carefully inserted the prongs into her mother's nostrils and turned the oxygen tank on. When Dr. Cuchinnati arrived it was to appear as though Lucy was so in shock that she left her mother untouched.

Number Five: Open window and release my soul.

Lucy opened the window next to the bed. Marge had told her to say a prayer for both of them. The *Million Dollar Movie* theme music came from the TV. Beyond the alley, in the moonlight, the clothesline shimmered, a shooting star against the cinder-block walls of the backyard. In the upper pane of glass, she could see her own dark reflection and the white brightness of the blankets behind her. If she stood perfectly still and concentrated hard enough, she thought she might see her mother's soul leaving her body.

"God forgive us," she whispered. A chill traveled up the length of her spine. Had her mother left? Turning away from the window, she watched her mother's motionless body. She grabbed the index cards and her mother's purse from the foot of the bed, then slowly backed into the kitchen.

Number Six: Call Dr. Cuchinnati.

The twenty-year-old bag was heavy, and camel-colored faux leather. Sometime during the seventies it was available for purchase exclusively on television. It had compartments specifically designed for a matching checkbook, address book, cigarette case, and key chain. When Marge saw it, she knew it was the perfect purse for her — a place for everything and everything in its place. The pages of the address book crinkled like old parchment from the stress of Marge's printing as Lucy searched for the doctor's information even though she knew the number. She needed the prop. The line rang and rang and Lucy envisioned the octogenarian slowly making his way to the telephone. Finally he answered. She could hear her mother's voice in her head as she recited her lines: "She went peacefully in her sleep during the eleven o'clock news. I called to her from the kitchen to see if she wanted anything and there was no answer."

*　　*　　*

With Marge's purse in tow and the index cards folded into her palm, Lucy went to the doctor on the front stoop. Being alone with her mother frightened her now, despite her years of practice keeping the dead company. Since the doctor lived several blocks away and stubbornly refused to take a taxi, Lucy knew she'd be waiting for some time while he hobbled over. The coolness of the marble step seeped through her threadbare sweatpants. She reached into her mother's purse and pulled out the matching cigarette case. Some of its color had crumbled away. Her hands trembled as she lit a cigarette. Then she began to pull at the hair on her forearm; the pain grounded her.

She looked over at the darkened row houses across the street. Her entire life had happened on this narrow street in South Philadelphia. She knew every neighbor, at least by sight. The houses were all the same — two-story red brick fronts, a bay window on the first floor, two windows on the second. Tonight, they resembled yawning faces. Some neighbors had opted to install aluminum siding over the brick front. Others stuck artificial grass to their steps, perhaps in an attempt to bring some green to the lawnless neighborhood. While Marge disapproved of these embellishments, her pet peeve was the adornment of the bay windows with Virgin Marys or cat and dog figurines or plastic flower arrangements against white vertical blinds. The

Pescitellis had sheer curtains and heavy, dark mustard-colored drapes. A single crystal lamp lit the window. On this night, many houses had seasonal cardboard decorations of ghosts, witches, and black cats taped to the windows.

Only a few trees were on the block. In front of their house, at the base of their stoop, was a square of mismatched cement. When her father lived in the house alone, before he'd met her mother, a tree grew there. In the spring, it produced white blossoms. Marge had it removed, fearing it would fall on the house or tangle its roots around the sewer pipe.

Lucy slipped off one of her black flats and stubbed out her cigarette in its soft foam sole, which, from wear, resembled a waffle. Marge didn't like marks from extinguished cigarettes on the sidewalk, and Lucy didn't want to re-enter the house alone to retrieve an ashtray. Through the vertical blinds, Lucy spied the purple-pink light of televisions in some of the houses.

The street was quiet. She lit another cigarette and stared at the burning embers and the smoke drifting up. Since it was Mischief Night, she thought she might see some kids making mischief. At twenty-nine, she'd never seen it happen. But every Halloween morning, without exception, she awoke to see soaped-up car windows and doorways and store fronts splattered with over-ripened tomatoes and raw eggs.

A couple approached; they weren't from the neighborhood.

"Those'll kill ya, ya know," the woman commented as they walked by.

"Yeah," Lucy said, "I know."

She took a deep drag, then blew the smoke out in a steady stream. So far the day had gone exactly as planned. In the morning she had finished some minor household tasks before the visitors for the day arrived. Fr. Reed heard Marge's confession, gave her Holy Communion, and seemed to suspect nothing out of the ordinary. Jack Kelleher arrived in the afternoon. Marge had respected and trusted Jack as a friend and a lawyer, because his aunt, Mrs. Garrity, who lived across the street, was her best friend. Jack was in his late thirties and had gone away for law school but returned to the neighborhood. Something graduates rarely did. He was the opposite of her sister Anne, who only returned for funerals.

Lucy lit another cigarette with the last one. The folded index cards were damp from being clenched in her fist. Despite this, the lines and dots Marge had embedded into the cards still felt like Braille. When Marge first reviewed them with her, Lucy felt demeaned by their simplicity and repetitiveness, but they had proven a comfort this night, allowing her to focus on tasks, not the implications of her actions. She unfolded them. The next card gave instructions for calling Anne. Lucy wasn't going to do this until Marge's body had been taken from the house. Marge didn't want Anne coming over and asking questions while she was still there. Lucy flipped to the last card.

Number Eight: Destroy To-Do list.

The final item.

St. Peter's loomed large over the squat houses. Its muted bell rang out midnight. Her cigarette had burned down to the filter; it singed her fingers. For a moment she absorbed the pain. Then she ground the butt into her shoe and shoved the cards into her pocket. The sound of footfalls echoed down the deserted street and Dr. Cuchinnati's elongated shadow appeared before he turned the corner.

Chapter Two

Joseph's family had embraced Dr. Cuchinnati as their doctor when he was first out of medical school. Lucy remembered him always looking the same as he did now, even though she'd known him since she was a child. In his trench coat, he resembled a taller, skinnier, though still hunched, version of Detective Columbo. The doctor grunted slightly as he entered the house. He had a habit of humming and grunting constantly — a very low soundtrack to his thoughts and movements. This night it made Lucy nervous. She hoped that he knew them too well to question what he saw before him. He seemed more distracted than usual though, not even noticing that Lucy carried a shoe filled with spent cigarettes. Perhaps this was how he was around death — oblivious, at least to Lucy, altogether.

When he reached Marge, he took his eyeglasses from the breast pocket of his coat and placed them on the tip of his nose. "Hmm," he mumbled. There was normally a shake to his hands so the sight of his trembling digits delicately removing her mother's tubing didn't alarm Lucy. He draped the tubing over the tank's gauge and turned off the oxygen. "Uh-huh." He raised his hand over Marge's face and for a moment Lucy thought he was going to give her mother a papal-like blessing. Instead, he rubbed the top of her head as though she were a small child clinging to his leg. It made Lucy uneasy to see her mother touched so intimately.

"She was a good girl. It's a shame she left us so soon." His hand swept down Marge's face and closed her eyelids. As he placed the sheet over

Marge's face, Lucy turned off the television.

"Well then, how about some coffee. It'll be a little while before Ralph gets here," he said, looking at Lucy for the first time. "Why the shoe?"

Lucy released a nervous laugh, shook her head in an attempt to appear calm, and limped into the kitchen. She dumped the ashes and butts into the trash can and rinsed her shoe under the faucet. The sole nearly detached and almost slid into the sink.

The doctor sat at the round table in his usual seat by the kitchen door, facing the window over the sink. She got the coffee started as he retrieved a slightly crumpled death certificate from the same breast pocket as his glasses. He unfolded it, then flattened it on the table. From the identical place, he took a pen. Lucy wondered at the size of the pocket. By this time, she had the mugs, cream, and sugar placed on the table and was seated beside him. The pen didn't work. He shook it and tried again. Finally, the ink came; it was blue. In his shaky penmanship he wrote her mother's name, each line a tiny vein. Quietly he hummed each letter, "*M*mmm, *A*aaaaa."

Lucy busied herself making coffee while they waited for Ralph. He was a co-worker from Anthony Botti's Funeral Home where Lucy worked part-time answering phones, typing invoices, and vacuuming and dusting a few evenings a week. Much of her time there, she spent alone or in the company of the deceased dressed up and waiting for their wakes the next day. Ralph interacted with both the living and the dead, doing pick-ups, acting as an usher, and driving the hearse to the cemetery. Everyone Lucy had ever known who died was buried out of Botti's. It was after her father's funeral that Mr. Botti offered her a position so that she could help out the family. She filled the mugs. "*R*rrrrr. *E*eeee." With her hands free from any other tasks, she gently tugged at her forearm hair.

When the car door slammed signaling Ralph's arrival, Lucy felt as if she'd been holding her breath for hours. It was almost over. Dr. Cuchinnati was nearly finished filling out the death certificate. Marge was on her way to Botti's. However, the sound of the car door slamming had not gone unnoticed on the block. As if insects heralded by a bug zapper, the street's blue-haired ladies flew from their homes, fumbling with the ties to their terrycloth robes, and landed on the Pescitellis' doorstep.

Ralph arrived in funeral director mode. He held Lucy's shoulders in a fatherly manner, telling her how sorry he was for her loss. Then the neighbors, led by Mrs. Garrity, attempted to slyly move her out of the dining room while Ralph prepared to remove Marge. Lucy didn't move. She wanted to see her mother's physical departure just as she'd witnessed her spiritual one. Ralph positioned the gurney next to the bed, then flung the body bag open as though it were a sheet. Awkwardly, in an almost violent act, he pulled Marge's upper body, then her lower body onto the bag. After tucking in her arms and legs, he pulled the zipper up to her neck, then looked to Lucy and asked if she wanted a minute with her mother. Lucy nodded. He joined the others in the kitchen.

The next time Lucy would see her mother she would be embalmed, painted, and dressed for burial — a corpse. Right now, she still resembled herself, wearing her nightgown, the softness of her skin intact. As Lucy leaned over and kissed her mother's forehead, she felt as though something had been unhinged deep within her. She was being shaken. She reached into her pocket and grasped the index cards. It was almost done. Just one more phone call to make.

Ralph returned to the room to take Marge. As he zipped the bag closed, Marge's hair caught in the zipper. He pulled back on the zipper and angled his back so that Lucy might not see the problem, but Lucy could see him press down on Marge's hair and zip the bag. The gurney thudded down each step — bang, bang, bang — as he wheeled her mother out of the house to the van, which was double-parked on the narrow street. And then they were gone.

In the kitchen, Lucy sat next to the doctor and watched as the older women swarmed about her mother's kitchen, cutting bread and cheese, gossiping about people from the neighborhood. This was the doctor's favorite kind of conversation. He would reveal all he knew with the exception of those things his profession required him to keep secret. Although, at times he would offer hypothetical scenarios without naming names. A plate of food appeared before Lucy. She sat watching them talk and eat; some did both simultaneously. Occasionally, one would touch her arm and whisper that everything would be all right. She didn't eat, couldn't eat, but she found their busyness, the clinking silverware, the thudding of mugs on the wood table comforting.

By noon the next day, everyone who'd known Marge would know of her death. The core group convened in the kitchen would spread the word at each of their errands, telling the butcher, the clerk at the post office, the grocer on the corner, and so on, until they returned in the late morning to light up the phone lines informing expatriates living in South Jersey. Their children, interrupted in the middle of their workdays, would politely express their condolences to their mothers. *But of course I remember Marge. Oh, really, she was that young? How sad.*

Lucy mumbled that she had a phone call to make and pulled Marge's purse onto her shoulder. Mrs. Garrity patted her hand, saying, "We'll be here." The din of the old ladies and the doctor chattering traveled through the house and upstairs to the front bedroom, Marge's room. Other than the kitchen, it was the only room with a phone. The mattress springs squeaked under Lucy's weight. She'd never spent any time in this room. The cherry bedroom set, which included the bureau, armoire, nightstands, and bed, was a wedding gift from Joseph. He'd wanted his bride to have a proper boudoir. Marge had never replaced anything in it, not even the mattress.

Number Seven: Call Margaret Anne.

Since she didn't know her sister's phone number by heart, Lucy referenced the pages of her mother's address book again and found Anne listed as Margaret Anne Pescitelli Anderson. During college, her sister had started using her middle name exclusively and never went back. Marge, not surprisingly, took it as an affront and in protest called her daughter Margaret Anne, as though she were perpetually in trouble. For Lucy it had been a hard adjustment to stop calling her sister Margie. She still paused before she addressed her to make sure she said Anne. People in the neighborhood still asked how little Margie was. Lucy never bothered to explain the name change, as it embarrassed her. She placed her hand on the phone but didn't lift the receiver. It was late, almost two a.m. Voices from downstairs filtered into her consciousness:

"She was in so much pain. Although she never showed it."

"God bless her."

"She's in heaven with Joseph now," said Mrs. Garrity, always the incurable romantic.

Lucy wasn't certain her mother was going to heaven after what they'd done. Her father was there. Of this, she was certain. When Lucy had asked her mother if she would go to hell for committing suicide, Marge told Lucy not to worry. She had it covered. Her logic was this: since Lucy killed her, she wasn't responsible herself and should enter heaven without complication. After her death Lucy was to confess the murder immediately, but preferably in a different parish. Marge didn't include this step on her index cards, which made Lucy wonder about her mother's concern for her immortal soul. And Lucy didn't believe that Marge was safe from eternal damnation, for she had masterminded the plan. She had forced Lucy to kill her. Had Marge confessed her plan to Fr. Reed that morning?

Her hand still resting on the phone, Lucy worried that her sister might be able to tell what had really happened just by hearing Lucy's voice. In the Pescitelli family, Anne was "the gifted child." She was smart, attractive, and athletic. With these attributes Anne would have been the favorite child of any mother, but not Marge. Her mother treated Anne's gifts as defects — too smart for her own good, obsessed with her appearance, and good at sports just so as not to be home. But that didn't mean that Lucy was Marge's favorite. Even though Lucy was loyal and obedient and appreciated her family, Marge found fault in her too. Things had to be done her way, to her standards. Standards that Lucy found hard to meet day in and day out. Lucy was average. There were no expectations, good or bad. Despite the fact that Anne never returned home after college, that Lucy didn't know her sister as an adult, she was still nervous that Anne might figure out that she'd killed their mother just by interpreting her quavering voice over the phone line.

Lucy ran her fingers over the seventh index card again. She lit a cigarette and placed it in the bedside ashtray. Someone picked up the phone, then dropped it. Anne's husband Brad grumbled into the phone. When he recognized it was Lucy, he expressed his hope that everything was all right and passed the phone to Anne.

"I'm sorry to be calling so late," Lucy said, not knowing how to continue.

"Is it Mom?" Anne sounded alert for just being awoken, as if she'd been expecting the call.

"Yes." Lucy rolled the cigarette along the rim of the ashtray.

"She's gone?"

"Yes." There was silence for a few moments. Lucy took a drag on the cigarette. "She went peacefully in her sleep during the eleven o'clock news. I called to her from the kitchen to see if she wanted anything and there was no answer." She exhaled the smoke.

"Are you okay?" Anne said.

"Sure, why?"

"Mom just died, Lucy. Why don't I come over? You shouldn't be alone tonight."

"No, that's okay. Really, I'm fine. The neighbors are here, so is Dr. Cuchinnati. Everything's being taken care of. I should probably go." She pulled the phone cord taut, nearly yanking it out of the receiver.

"I'll come in the morning. Try to sleep, if you can," Anne said.

"Thanks. Goodnight."

After Lucy hung up, she sat going over the conversation in her head, hoping she hadn't said anything wrong.

*   *   *

The next morning Lucy woke up on the couch, her face stuck to the plastic covering, and a crocheted afghan thrown over her. She was disoriented, forgetting she had retreated to the living room sometime after three in the morning, forgetting she was alone. The phone was ringing. She trudged to the kitchen and picked it up. It was Anne saying she was heading over and would be there in about forty minutes. Lucy hung up, leaned into the dining room, and said, "That was Margaret Anne, she's on her way. . . ." Her eyes focused; the hospital bed was empty. The TV stand had been pushed aside to make room for the gurney, but everything else was as it had been for months.

Lucy turned and collapsed into a chair and saw that the kitchen was immaculate. The counter was cleared and cleaned, the dishes in the cabinets, the spices in their rack above the stove. It was as if these ladies' kitchens were set up in an identical fashion to Marge's — a universal rule of organization established to insure any woman could walk into another's kitchen, prepare and serve a meal, and then leave it exactly as she had found it. Her mother would have been pleased with the neighbors' respectful treatment of her home.

She had left her mother's last pack of cigarettes in the kitchen the night before and she found it resting in a clean ashtray in the center of the table, the lighter on top of it. She rubbed her forearms and then reached for the pack. Only one smoke remained. She pulled it out, then flattened the cardboard box, folded it, and put in her pocket. There was a full carton in the cabinet next to the cleaning supplies. Lucy held the cigarette in front of her with both hands. No one her age smoked the long brown cigarettes but her, and she smoked them because Marge had. When she had started smoking as a teenager, she only smoked at home. It happened by accident, really. One Saturday morning at the breakfast table while she waited for her eggs, Lucy had mindlessly taken a smoke from her mother's pack and tapped its filter on the table, as she'd seen her mother do. She twirled it like a miniature baton between her fingers, then put it in her mouth just as Marge turned to slide the eggs from the frying pan to her daughter's plate.

"Oh, for chrissake." Marge returned the pan to the stove, took the cigarette out of Lucy's mouth, turned it around, and put it back in. "You got it in backwards." Marge lit Lucy's cigarette and said, "Don't flick ash in your eggs."

With the end of her sleeve, Lucy dabbed her eyes, then pinched her nose. She smoked her mother's last cigarette. She knew she should quit now, particularly with her mother dead, dead from lung cancer. While Marge was alive, Lucy felt that this habit was one of the few things they shared. The house was quiet without the sound of her mother's coughing and gagging in the next room.

On the windowsill above the sink, where the white curtains embroidered with the gold and brown were pulled to either side, Marge's recipe box sat centered in the middle, like a tabernacle upon an altar. The morning sun reflected off the lid of the olive-green metal box. It contained five-by-seven index cards with lists of chores per day and her mother's instructions on how to do everything from scrubbing the toilet to making gravy to flossing teeth. It also held cards with Marge's specific directions about how things should proceed after her death in the few days before she was buried. The smoke from Lucy's cigarette swirled and floated, forming ghostly images in the morning sunlight. She finished the cigarette and cleaned out the ashtray.

A knock on the front door startled Lucy. Stacks of index cards from the box were on the table in front of her; one stack for Marge's obituary, one for her funeral arrangements, another for food preparations for guests coming back to the house, etc. The ashtray was nearly full. Lucy hadn't even noticed. She'd meant to take a shower and get dressed before her sister arrived. As she got up to clean the ashtray, she heard the door open.

"Lucy?"

"In here."

Anne stood in the kitchen doorway. "Did you hear me knock? Are you okay?" Then, not waiting for an answer, "You look like hell." She walked past her sister and opened the kitchen window.

"Thanks," Lucy said.

"Were you able to get any sleep?" Anne waved her hands about, directing the cloud of smoke toward the window.

"A few hours on the couch."

"We couldn't find a parking space anywhere. Brad had to drop me off. He's parking at the ACME."

Lucy wasn't surprised. When Anne did visit, this topic was always the opener. She wondered why they didn't just park at the ACME in the first place instead of trolling around the narrow streets in their mammoth SUV.

"There's coffee," Lucy said.

"Thanks. But I don't drink coffee. Remember? Do you have tea?" Anne said.

"Yeah, I think there's some." Lucy felt something scratch her leg. She reached into her pocket assuming it was the cigarette box but discovered instead the index cards with Marge's final to-do list. The box was in her other pocket. She looked quickly at her sister as she crumbled the cards with her fist and pushed them further into her pocket.

Anne stood at the counter. After a moment, she began opening cabinets. Lucy saw her searching and pointed to one of the cabinets.

"Tea's in there. Lipton, nothing fancy. Cups are over there. Kettle's on the stove."

"I can find the kettle. Sorry," Anne said. "I haven't lived here for a long time."

"Everything's the same."

Lucy poured herself some coffee. Sitting, she could feel the cards against her leg. She lit a cigarette. When was the last time she was alone in a room with her sister? Already, she and Anne were falling into their usual routine of established impatience. She wasn't sure when they'd started being this way with each other but it was before Anne had left for college, after their father had died. They took out their frustrations with their mother on each other, knowing it was safer than confronting Marge.

After retrieving a teabag and a cup, Anne put the kettle on and joined her sister at the kitchen table. She sat opposite Lucy, occasionally waving the smoke away from her. She regarded the index cards with recognition and asked if all the arrangements were made at Botti's and what else needed to be done. Of course, everything had been taken care of, except for a few errands. The hospital bed needed to be sent back and the dining room returned to its former state. Marge's outfit had to be taken to the funeral home. Food needed to be purchased and prepared. One of them would need to call in the obituary. Anne volunteered to write it. Lucy handed her the pile of index cards, explaining that it was already written, and that the phone numbers of the *Philadelphia Inquirer* and *Daily News* were on the last card. Anne read silently and shook her head.

Anne's hair was pulled back into a barrette at the base of her head; her freckles were covered up by expensive-smelling foundation. She had Marge's profile.

She took care of herself, still running and swimming regularly. Exercise had never appealed to Lucy. If she pulled her dark black hair back, it was in a high ponytail. There were times when she considered emulating her sister, but laziness and indifference kept her from doing anything. Besides, Marge had always said it was a sign of vanity to spend so much time on yourself.

"I'm not calling this in. I couldn't do it with a straight face. 'Margaret Pescitelli. A Life of Giving.' Come on." Anne lightly tossed the cards on the table. "I'll write something."

"You will not. I'll call it in if it's too much for you to do for your own mother," Lucy countered.

"Have you even read it?" The kettle whistled; Anne turned off the stove.

"Well, obviously I will when I call it in." Lucy lit another cigarette; she wanted to create distance between herself and her sister. They said nothing as Anne prepared her tea.

Brad called in through the screen door. "Lucy? Anne? Is this the right place?" In the past he'd commented that all the row houses in South Philadelphia looked the same. Lucy felt the same way about the houses in their South Jersey development.

Brad was too polite to enter on his own. Lucy walked through the darkened living room and squinted as she opened the door for him. Once she let him in, it took her eyes a moment to adjust and focus on him. She didn't see him bending down to kiss her cheek and it startled her.

"Good morning, Lucy. I'm so sorry for your loss," he said. "Please let me assist you in any way. I'm sure there are many details to take care of and this is a stressful and emotional time . . ."

"Enough," Anne said, as she walked into the living room. Lucy assumed she was speaking to her until she noticed Brad take on the posture of the reprimanded. Anne didn't normally speak to Brad like he was family.

"Thanks, Brad. You're very nice." Lucy said, almost as an antidote to her sister's harshness. Lucy liked Brad even though Marge had not. He always tried to say the right thing but in a very long way. His occupation was something very corporate, senior level, but Lucy always lost interest soon after he started describing what he did for a living. The first time she'd met Brad was the day after her father died. However, the family had heard of Brad before that, as Anne had opted to spend the Columbus Day holiday with the Andersons rather than her own family.

Anne and Brad volunteered to buy the groceries since they were already parked at the supermarket. It was decided that Lucy would prepare the house for company and call in the obit (which she did find a little embarrassing). First she went to the kitchen and emptied bags of Halloween candy into a large bowl. Marge insisted that the neighborhood children not be denied their candy. Things still had to be taken care of.

Lucy set the candy bowl on the end table by the door and went upstairs. She pulled out Marge's last cigarette pack from one pant pocket, the index cards from the other. A jewelry box she had had since she was a child sat on the chest of drawers. When it was open a plastic ballerina dressed in a pink tutu spun as a tinny "Somewhere over the Rainbow" played. Lucy pushed the folded cigarette pack into one compartment, the crushed index cards into another. The music came to a slow stop as she closed the lid.

Chapter Three

The familiar smells of floral wreaths, white candles, and disinfectant air freshener pervaded the large parlor of the funeral home. Anthony Botti, Sr., stood at the head of Marge's coffin directing the mourners. He'd come out of retirement for today's service, more out of affection for Lucy's father than respect for her mother. This was the first time in a dozen years that Lucy was here in the morning, and the room seemed less reverent without the softening shadows cast by the standing lamps. In the evenings, she never witnessed the deceased being chaperoned from the building, and for this she was grateful; she hated seeing coffin lids close.

Lucy sat with Anne and Brad on the stiff upholstered couch opposite her mother's open coffin. Her parents' wedding photo was propped on the quilted lid of the casket. From the living room wall, Lucy had taken the black-and-white image from where it hung between JFK and Pope John Paul II and above Lucy's and Anne's First Holy Communion pictures. Joseph and Marge stood outside of Saint Peter's Church, the same church where the funeral mass would be celebrated shortly. From the gold frame, the two peered into their shared future. Joseph smiled broadly, squinting into the sunlight, while Marge stood brave under the weight of her husband's arm. In her white-gloved hands, she held tight to a small bouquet of roses.

Brad held Anne's hand in his, stroking it with his thumb. From the time her sister was in high school, she was like a captured panther exhausting its pent-up energy pacing its cage, chewing on its provided meat with disdain, and eyeing its keepers as they latched the gate. She'd distanced herself from Marge, so now she didn't have to worry about being convicted of murder or burning in hell. Lucy envied Anne's having someone here to console her. She didn't even love Marge. Yet, there was Brad sitting next to her, standing when she stood, fetching her a glass of water, and, Lucy imagined, holding her through the night.

Lucy surveyed the plaster ceiling of the room, noticing tiny cracks emanating from the chandelier ceiling plate. A corner tip of one sheet of wallpaper was peeling away from its adjacent partner. The tiny floral print no longer aligned. Life at home had been comfortable for her, and Lucy found that agreeing with her mother had made her mother an agreeable companion. At some point, she'd forgotten to develop her own expectations. When had she accepted that being with Marge, being alone, was acceptable? Now, she alone bore the family's sins and crimes.

The temperature had dropped overnight and it was cooler, despite the bright sun. The light shone through the sheer white curtains and Lucy could see dust motes floating in the air. As mourners approached her to express their condolences, light radiated from behind them. Each time, Lucy positioned herself so that their bodies blocked the sun from her eyes until they moved on to offer a final prayer at the side of the coffin. Some people patted Marge's hands as they stood or knelt, but everyone was reserved. At her father's funeral almost everyone had kissed him. Mr. Botti had to touch up his face makeup to cover all the lipstick marks.

Occasionally above the quiet murmuring, they talked for Lucy's benefit and Lucy would nod and smile, despite her desire to leave the room. *So few people are allowed to die at home these days. How wonderful to have a daughter to take care of you in your final hours. Marge was so fortunate to have a loyal daughter.*

Lucy longed for her mother to be in the ground, for the day to be over, hoping that perhaps her feelings of guilt might diminish once she was alone. She'd be alone with her sin. Her mother was different dead, less trustworthy. Lucy swore to keep the murder a secret, but looking back, she realized that her mother had never given her the same guarantee. Had Marge told anyone of her plan? Fr. Reed? Mrs. Garrity? Were there people, shifting quietly in their folding chairs, watching Lucy with the knowledge that she was a murderer?

Anne grabbed Lucy's hand.

"When are you going to stop that?" her sister said.

Lucy hadn't realized she'd been tugging on her forearm hair again. She pulled her hand from her sister and got up to pull down the shades. The room turned gray.

Glenn Lepper arrived with his mother on his arm. They snaked through the narrow aisles toward the front of the room to pay their respects to Marge. Mrs. Lepper was a kind woman, as far as Lucy could tell, attending every neighborhood funeral, presenting a strudel to each grieving household. She spoke very little English and often Glenn, perpetually by her side, bent to hear her and then translate a heartfelt sentiment on her behalf. Her face was that of a woman who baked, soft and malleable-looking, folding gently into her neck, slightly pale as if sprinkled with flour, filled with expressions of sweetness. And Glenn looked like one of her creations. His soft dimpled skin wrapped around thick solid bones seemed kneaded into place by his mother's short dexterous fingers.

Years ago, Mrs. Garrity and some of the neighbor women had proposed that Glenn and Lucy were a good match. Apparently, the one thing they had in common, still living with their mothers, made for a strong foundation. Marge immediately objected. She had no intentions of sharing a home with Mrs. Lepper. The conversation had made Lucy realize that people did pair her and Glenn in their minds, solely because they lived with their mothers. It was more unusual than it once had been. Glenn took care of his widowed mother; he worked full-time as a SEPTA bus driver to provide for her. People thought it strange that he didn't pursue a wife or get his own place. They thought there had to be something wrong with him. People must have thought the same of Lucy. Maybe they thought worse of her. Anyone who knew them knew that Lucy didn't provide for Marge, and didn't take care of her until the very end. A single woman, almost thirty, living with her mother, working part-time at a funeral home. Lucy closed her eyes. What did people say about her?

She returned to the couch where the three of them alone represented the family. Anne and Lucy were now truly orphans. Joseph's mother died in childbirth and his father, who never remarried, died before his grandchildren were born. Joseph adored his dead mother for sacrificing her life. To him, motherhood was the equivalent of sainthood. He'd been so grateful to Marge for giving him two children and surviving each birth.

After Marge married Joseph, her family disowned her. There was no attempt at reconciliation from either side. From her daily review of the obituaries, Marge knew both her parents were dead. She had three older brothers, but Anne and Lucy had never met them or even seen pictures. Still, Lucy looked around the room in search of men in their fifties or sixties whom she'd never seen before and who looked as if they were Marge's brothers. But every face was recognizable. Lucy had never gotten a straight answer from her mother about what had happened. Occasionally when pressed for a reason, Marge would say that her Irish family disapproved of Marge and Joseph's interracial marriage. Joseph was Italian. While Lucy thought the sarcastic remark held some truth, she also thought there had to be more to it.

A woman suddenly appeared in the doorway of the parlor and called across the room as though she were at a New Year's Eve party. "Little

Margie? Is that you?" It was their old neighbor Mrs. Clarke, who had moved to Boston to be near her son and his family.

"Oh no," Anne said under her breath, "it's Mrs. Whatshername from across the street."

Mrs. Clarke wasn't the first person to call Anne that; it had happened more than a few times in the past two days. When she remembered, Lucy had made a point of reintroducing her sister to people as Anne. Mrs. Clarke leaned over to hug and kiss Anne.

"When was the last time I saw you? You are the spitting image of your mother. God rest her soul."

"Thanks," Anne said. The woman looked at Brad. Anne introduced them. As Mrs. Clarke leaned to kiss his cheek, Brad stood to shake her hand. His forehead caught her chin. They both mumbled apologies, then she moved down the line.

After kissing Lucy on the cheek, she said, "It's what she wanted. She's with your father now." Was there a wink? Lucy wasn't sure as she watched Mrs. Clarke turn away and kneel at the coffin. Would Marge have called Mrs. Clarke? A long distance call?

When Anne excused herself and went to the bathroom, Brad slid over next to Lucy. He had nice features, but his hair was light blond and, from a distance, he looked as though he didn't have eyelashes or eyebrows. His skin was tan and looked older than its thirty-five years.

"I'm so proud of Anne. Despite the strained, sometimes volatile, relationship she had with her mother, she was there in the end. She's here today. So many children would have just walked away and not looked back. Don't you agree?" he said.

Lucy nodded and continued looking forward at the coffin. She felt uncomfortable facing someone sitting so close to her, particularly a man.

"And you, Lucy. You are so strong. I can't imagine enduring such tragedy as losing a parent. And you've lost both."

"Thank you, Brad."

"I hope this isn't inappropriate but all these years I have wanted to apologize for my part in the incident at your father's funeral. I had only just met Anne and I didn't know how to respond. You understand that I had to follow her lead?"

"Sure, Brad. Don't worry about it. That was so long ago."

When Joseph died, Anne had brought Brad home for the first time. At the wake, Anne and Marge had a huge argument when Anne insisted that Brad stay overnight in their house, in her bed. Marge refused. Anne left with Brad following and didn't return for her father's funeral mass or burial.

"You're very forgiving," he said. "I only wish I had said something to your mother. I felt uncomfortable bringing the topic up and I thought that maybe it was best left alone. I always wondered if your mother could have ever trusted me after that."

Marge believed Brad to be weak. She also thought that Anne was setting herself up for disappointment, putting too much faith in his ability to give her everything in life she wanted.

Jack Kelleher arrived and walked directly to Lucy. Along the way, he picked up a folding chair and placed it next to her. He kissed her on the cheek, then shook Brad's hand. Jack was a few years older than her brother-in-law and had light brown hair that was graying. His build was broader and shorter than Brad's. His presence relaxed Lucy. While she liked her brother-in-law, the way he talked about things openly and sincerely made her uneasy. She wondered how Anne could stand it. Jack, on the other hand, was family. He understood.

"Sorry I'm running late," Jack said, "Is Father starting soon?"

"In a few minutes," Lucy said.

Once Anne returned, Mr. Botti announced Fr. Reed had a few words to say. After the priest said a prayer, Mr. Botti asked any friends of the family to come forward and say their final farewells. When only Lucy, Anne, Brad, and Jack were left in the room with the funeral director, Jack approached Marge. He knelt, crossed himself, and bowed his head in prayer momentarily. Then he raised his head to look at Marge. A subtle laugh came from him as he shook his head. "I'm actually gonna miss you, Marge," he said as he gently palmed her hands. Anne and Brad stood a short distance from the kneeler in front of Marge's coffin and viewed her from there. They made an attractive couple, both of them fair, tall, and athletic. After a few moments, Anne turned away and Brad nodded to Mr. Botti as though approving a bottle of wine.

Mr. Botti took Marge and Joseph's wedding picture from its perch, then handed Lucy a white quilted blanket. It was soft in her hands as she carefully spread it across her mother's still body, as though covering a sleeping child. She tucked it around Marge's elbows and legs. The sight of her mother's feet, which abutted the casket and stood erect, alarmed her momentarily. As she draped the blanket over her mother's black low-heeled shoes, she had the desire to take them off, make her mother more comfortable. Marge's face no longer had that faded, well-scrubbed look. Mr. Botti had smoothed makeup over her skin, rouged her cheeks. And even though he had used Marge's own lipstick, he had put too much on her. Lucy bent to kiss her on the forehead, just as she had done that night. She whispered, "It's done." Then, remembering the to-do list in her jewelry box, she said, "Almost."

The sensation of being rattled from inside returned to her and she tightly gripped the side of the casket for support. A soft growl or moan started in her chest and she didn't recognize it as her own. Her hands wanted to flip the casket over, her legs wanted to climb in. Suddenly Jack held her shoulders, as if he knew she was on the verge of something.

Marge had hidden her pain, letting the cancer claim territory after territory within her, until Lucy came home from work one night. A PBS mystery was on the television, but Lucy could feel a quietness, a stillness, the instant she walked through the door. She discovered her mother collapsed in the kitchen doorway. In her hand, Marge held the amber ashtray that sat in the stand next to her recliner. She had just finished washing it. Lucy couldn't recall ever seeing her mother lie down before.

After a few moments, Jack turned Lucy away from her mother and handed her a handkerchief. When Lucy looked up, she saw Anne and Brad standing there, looking at her with sympathy. Anne appeared to have been crying, and Brad stood behind her holding her shoulders. Lucy wondered if he was mimicking Jack.

*　*　*

St. Peter's was a miniature cathedral, with marble pillars and oil paintings on the ceiling and behind the altar. The Stations of the Cross were depicted on the side walls in painted wood carvings. Her father had been baptized, married, and buried from St. Peter's. Lucy knew other religions looked down on the ornateness of Catholic churches, but she felt her father and her mother deserved such grandeur in their lives. This church was built with immigrant labor for their descendants to have a place to celebrate their lives. Why should this type of beauty be reserved for royalty or the rich? Why not a framer? A housewife?

As the priest descended from the altar to distribute Communion, the organist began playing "Ave Maria." The sound of the first few notes soothed Lucy. It was Marge's favorite song; "And such a Catholic song," she'd say, "not like 'Amazing Grace.' The Protestants love that one." The cantor's voice was beautiful. Brad seemed to be enjoying the Mass. At one point, he turned to Lucy and said, "This is quite beautiful. Charming, really." He and Anne sat with Lucy in the front row on the left side, facing the statue of the Blessed Mother. When Lucy rose to receive Communion, Brad followed suit.

"That's not for you." Anne remained seated as she pulled her husband back into the pew.

It wasn't for Lucy on this day either, not with a mortal sin on her soul. She felt guilty receiving Communion; she hadn't been to confession first. Wasn't that another mortal sin? She was tallying them up. But people would notice if she didn't and be suspicious. She took the long way back to her seat, across the front of the church, down the side aisle, and into the opposite end of the pew. Her mouth felt parched and the Host was difficult to swallow. She knelt next to her sister.

Lucy couldn't remember the last time they'd been in church together. There were definite signs that Anne was pulling away from the family and the Church even before Joseph's death. As Lucy watched her neighbors file up the aisle, pass Marge's closed coffin, and receive Communion, she remembered another time.

Lucy had been in eighth grade. Her class was studying World War II. One night, she was stretched out on the living room floor in front of the television with her history textbook opened to a map of Europe that covered both pages. She was trying to memorize the location of the countries during commercials. Marge sat in her chair, the brown and cream upholstered recliner, watching the eleven o'clock news when suddenly she yelled, "What on earth?"

Lucy looked up to see Anne on the television. An on-screen banner under her image read "Protester" and she held a sign that said "Choice."

"Oh, no. Not my daughter." Marge yelled up the stairs toward Anne's room, "Margaret Anne!"

Lucy sat up, her eyes back on the screen. Anne's image was gone. Lucy was certain that the entire neighborhood had heard her mother's shrill cry. She imagined them perched at their windows, straining to hear the impending argument.

"Wha . . . at?!" Anne responded in kind from her room.

"Get down here." Marge's eyes scanned the ceiling; she listened for any sound of movement, her hands fused to her hips.

Finally Anne came thundering down the steps. "Wha . . . at?"

"What the hell is this? Is this where you were? You said you were at a track meet," Marge said, as she pointed at the television, which was now showing a commercial for toilet bowl cleaner.

Anne looked at her mother, then at the television. "What are you talking about?"

"We saw you on the news. Protesting! I'm sure everyone saw you." Marge responded without looking at the television. "Do you even know what it means?"

Anne's mouth hung open. Her body swayed as she held tight to the banister. She hadn't expected to get caught, but she didn't back down. Calmly, she said, "Women should have the right to choose."

"To kill their babies?" Marge said.

"It's not killing. They're not born yet."

"So they're not people."

"Exactly."

"So if I'd gotten rid of you. It wouldn't have meant anything." Marge's hand went to her forehead as if checking herself for a fever. "It doesn't mean anything to you that you wouldn't be here to have this argument with me."

"I wouldn't know the difference," Anne said.

Lucy could tell that as her mother grew quieter she grew angrier. Her sister didn't seem to have the same realization.

"Women are liberated now. We don't have to have children we don't want."

"So being liberated means you can get pregnant? Anyone can do that!" Marge said.

"No. It means I don't have to keep a baby I don't want."

Lucy watched in amazement as Marge turned away from Anne, grabbed her purse and left the house. The sisters looked at each other; their mother never walked away from a confrontation. Lucy wanted to say something but was too shocked. Shocked that her mother left, shocked that Anne was on television, shocked that Anne thought about being pro-choice at all.

Anne went back upstairs to her bedroom. Lucy waited up on the couch, finally falling asleep. When Joseph returned from the Phillies' game, which had gone into extra innings, he sent her to bed. Her mother was probably at Mrs. Garrity's, he told her, "Not to worry."

Marge woke Lucy the next morning for school. The silence at the kitchen table made it difficult for Lucy to swallow her instant oatmeal. At school, first thing, she was called into the principal's office. Sister Paul Michael didn't look up from her desk when Lucy was nudged into the room or while she stood silent and waited. Sister had the rosary in her right hand; it was her way of calming herself and asking for insight she said. Occasionally, she released an exasperated exhale. Lucy assumed Sister Paul was Italian and much older than her mother. Most everyone Lucy knew was either Italian or Irish. She couldn't be sure about the nun's age, since she couldn't see any hair, gray or otherwise, sneaking out the edges of her black habit.

"Sit." Sister Paul placed her rosary on the desk.

Lucy sat with her hands folded in her lap.

"Do you share your sister's view of abortion, young lady?"

"No, Sister."

"I would hope not. You're a good child. Some of us have thought that you might even receive the calling to join the order. God willing."

"Yes, Sister." Lucy had considered being a nun, but at thirteen, the idea of being a saint or even a martyr interested her more.

"Perhaps, you can consider this an opportunity to act on God's behalf and show your sister the truth." Sister Paul Michael pulled a rolled-up poster from the metal credenza behind her desk. Carefully, she removed the tape and unraveled the poster. Lucy recognized it immediately; she had sat next to it throughout the seventh grade. Babies. Dead babies. The aftermath of several types of abortions were documented in color photography. The photos of the salt solution and vacuum abortions were the most horrifying. Despite her familiarity with the pictures, Lucy was repulsed. The poor babies. How could Anne think this was okay?

Lucy carried the poster home after school. This could be her first act toward sainthood. She would convince her sister that she was wrong, that abortion was murder. The rolled-up poster was Lucy's lightsaber and with it she would conquer evil. Some of the neighborhood boys began to chase her down the street, screaming, "Baby killer!" When she reached her stoop, she turned and faced them, brandishing her poster, and yelled, "Am not!" It seemed everyone in the parish watched Channel 6 News.

Lucy went upstairs, her weapon unrolled now, and pushed her sister's door open.

"Anne. Look at this," Lucy said, shielded by the paper.

"Get that thing out of here." Anne tore the poster from her hands and crumpled it. "They're just trying to scare you, Lucy, to brainwash you." She pushed her little sister from her room and slammed the door shut. Her shout was muffled, "When are you going to start thinking for yourself?"

That day Anne was called to her principal's office too. After defending her actions, she was expelled from school. Everyone knew. No parents wanted their children anywhere near Anne. She finished school at the public high school, which was considered the diocese's dumping ground for troublemakers and kids who flunked out.

Lucy never confronted her sister on the issue again, just as her mother hadn't. They didn't talk about it for the same reason — the fear that maybe Anne had had an abortion and that forcing the issue would produce an admission from her. Neither one could deal with it. That day Lucy felt that she had to choose between her mother and her sister. While she knew she had failed in her attempt at sainthood, she felt certain she had taken the right moral stand and that her mother would appreciate her efforts.

*   *   *

Lucy knelt by the glass coffee table, slowly wiping away the Windex, while her sister and Brad washed the dishes in the kitchen. All the guests were gone, even Mrs. Garrity. There were no index cards with instructions on what to do now that Marge was buried. Anne came into the living room, drying her hands with the dishtowel.

"I think that's everything," she said. "Is there anything else we can do before we head out?"

"No," Lucy said, turning to inspect the plastic couch cover for any spots.

"Why don't you stay with us awhile?" Anne put the towel over her shoulder, something Marge used to do, and Lucy wondered if her sister realized.

"I'll be fine. I've got work tomorrow anyway." She stood and walked into the kitchen. Brad moved out of her way as she put the cleaner under the sink and threw the crumpled moist paper towels in the trash.

"Are you sure you want to go back to the funeral home?" Anne leaned in the doorway. "So soon?"

"It's my job," Lucy said. The dishes were drying in the rack and Lucy was grateful that Anne and Brad hadn't attempted to put them away; she wouldn't have been able to find anything the next day. She felt ready to be alone.

"Okay. But come over to our house for dinner next week. Or spend the weekend," Anne said.

"I could come get you," Brad volunteered. By now, he was standing behind Anne, that much closer to the front door.

"Sure," Lucy said, walking past them. As she opened the front door, Anne searched for her purse. Lucy had been at their house in New Jersey once.

After she watched them walk down the block, she locked the front door and went to her bedroom. She took Marge's holy card from her pocket before she sat on the bed. The Blessed Mother stood serenely, palms facing out, crushing the serpent under her feet. For years, Lucy had collected holy cards. She opened the drawer of her nightstand where, among others, there were several cards just like this one. She ran her fingers over their smooth matte finishes. There was Saint Francis of Assisi surrounded by animals, The Holy Ghost represented by a soaring dove, and Jesus kneeling, hands together, under shafts of light from a divine cloud. Lucy closed the drawer, deciding instead, to place Marge's Blessed Mother in the care of her jewelry box.

Chapter Four

As Lucy sat in Jack Kelleher's makeshift office waiting for Anne and Brad to arrive, waiting for Jack to return from the back with coffee, she could feel the nervousness building beneath her damp skin. The office was an old storefront, formerly a butcher shop. The desk, filing cabinets, and chairs were crowded into the front room of the building where customers used to wait with numbered paper tags. Between the wooden furniture and the counter hung a thick plastic sheet. The wall separating the front room from the back was demolished except for the studs. Lucy suspected animals had been slaughtered, or at the very least cut into pieces, in this room.

Ten days ago Marge was buried, but her funeral hadn't brought the peace or the finality that Lucy had assumed it would. This morning Jack would read her mother's will. She worried that Marge had left some final words, perhaps a last-minute confession detailing the crime. The night before when she finally drifted off to sleep, Lucy dreamt that her mother, in all her ghostly glory, stood next to her bed. She wasn't alone. Beside her stood Columbo, smoking his cigar and jotting down observations in his notepad. Marge handed him an ashtray. Behind him, appearing as his elongated shadow, was Dr. Cuchinnati. Marge held a pillow and explained the simplicity, the ingenuity of her plan. Apparently, she felt the need to brag in the afterlife. Then, in demonstration, she placed the pillow over Lucy's face and pressed down. Lucy awoke out of breath with her pillow over her face. She grabbed the pillow and threw it into the hallway. No one was there. Then she got up to slam the door. Was it a dream or was her mother haunting her? She thought of the evidence in her jewelry box. Was Marge somehow aware that Lucy had not destroyed the index cards?

On her way to Jack's — and it was not her imagination — rain began to pour down as she passed St. Peter's Church. A sun shower. In November. Weighted down by her soaked clothing, she felt sin-laden.

By the time Jack returned with the coffee, Lucy's forearms were pink with anxiety. She exchanged the towel he'd given her when she arrived for a mug.

"I didn't know we were supposed to get rain today." He draped the towel over the back of his chair, then searched for a spot on the desk to put his mug. "I found some tea for Anne, just in case. What do you think is taking them so long?"

"Parking."

"Why don't they just park at the ACME?" He moved dust-covered piles of paint brochures, wood-floor samples, blueprints, and fabric swatches to the floor behind him.

"I know," Lucy said. "I guess Anne thinks it isn't right to park there if you're not shopping there."

"So what do you think?" he said, waving his hand toward the back of the building. "It's got real potential. Don't you think?"

"I guess. It just seems like a lot of work. Couldn't you have just rented an office?"

"Where's the fun in that? Besides I like a challenge, the idea of making this my own unique place."

"Well, it is that." Lucy pulled her pant leg from her skin.

"I think it should express who I am not only as a lawyer but as a person."

"Uh-huh." Lucy was unconvinced that the butcher shop would ever represent Jack.

"Besides change is good for the soul."

Anne and Brad knocked. Jack led them in, apologizing for the mess, describing it as a work-in-progress.

Marge had written a letter to be read at this time. Jack opened it with a dull envelope opener that bunched up the final corner. From the envelope he pulled a slim stack of index cards. At the sight of her mother's print-ing through the back of the last card, Lucy worried that her mother might reveal all. She glanced at Jack and Anne and Brad. What would these three do? She imagined Anne's sense of justice forcing her to ensure that her sister paid her debt to society — family be damned; Jack legally obliged to call the police; Brad promising to get her the best defense his money could buy; and then Jack taking offence and demanding that only he could represent her. He'd visit her on holidays with appropriate convict presents: cigarettes, magazines, but never a nail file. Maybe it wouldn't be so bad. Maybe the din of the prisoners talking throughout the night, and the smell of smoke wafting through the cinder-block hallways would lull her to sleep, a deep sleep with no ghostly visitations.

Marge's letter started the same as her correspondence to school principals, gym coaches, and teachers had always begun, which made Lucy wonder who her mother imagined would be present. Did she expect that this final communication would be read again and again in the courtroom? Printed in the paper?

> To Whom It May Concern:
>
> I've asked my attorney John Kelleher, Esquire, to read this letter as the executor of my last will and testament. I expect that both my daughters, Lucretia Maria Pescitelli and Margaret Anne Pescitelli Anderson, along with her husband, Brad Anderson, are present.
>
> I will make this brief in the interest of time, my time. All the details are in my will. The house has been promised to the Archdiocese of Philadelphia upon my death. The mortgage has been paid off for many years now. The taxes are up to date. I have left my savings to Lucy to do with as she wishes. This money could help purchase another house. However, I have always felt that Lucy should consider a religious order. The Sisters of Saint Joseph were always fond of her. I believe the lifestyle would suit her as well, although they may require her to quit smoking. The contents of the house, with the exception of a few items I've left for the neighbors, are to go solely to Lucy.
>
> To Anne, and her husband Brad, I leave nothing. Anne decided long ago that she neither needed nor wanted anything from me, so I will not burden her with anything of mine.
>
> I tried my best with you girls. The rest is up to you.
> Sincerely,
> Margaret Anne Pescitelli

When there was no response, Jack cleared his throat. There was a layer of white dust on his desk and Lucy wondered if it was just plaster or if animal remains — bones, feathers, teeth — were intermingled. Marge had not revealed her as a murderer, hadn't even hinted at it. But had she heard correctly? Her mother had given away their home, Lucy's only home. Something about nuns?

John reordered the cards, tapped them against his desktop, as if they were playing cards.

"Well," he began.

"Lucy did she tell you any of this?" Anne interrupted. One hand gripped the arm of Lucy's chair. The other, Brad held tightly.

Lucy shook her head, her eyes on Jack.

"I couldn't say anything. I'm sorry. Your mother was my client," he said, putting the cards back in the ripped envelope.

"She was insane," Anne said.

Everyone was looking at Lucy. "Excuse me for a moment," she said. Behind the thick plastic, she lit a cigarette while the three of them remained in their chairs. She inhaled deeply. No jail time. It would seem. But homeless. Thrown out on the street by her mother. What had she done to deserve this? She exhaled. She'd done everything her mother had asked of her. As she paced in the small space between the dirty glass counter and the tiled wall, it occured to her — this is how her mother had it covered. She had purchased God's forgiveness. Did she really think giving the Church the house would save her soul? And did it?

On the other side of the plastic, Jack had given Anne her copy of the will.

"I don't see why I need a copy," Anne said. "I think she pretty much summed it up in the note."

"Are you okay?" Jack asked.

"Sure." Anne waved him off with one of the few gestures she had in common with Marge, since she'd never taken up smoking.

"Of course she's not," Brad said, taking Anne's hand into both of his. "It's inconceivable that she could be. Her mother's practically disowned her from the grave. It's unforgivable."

"Please Brad. You knew my mother."

"Marge was in a lot of pain at the end," Jack said.

"Are you saying that she wasn't of sound mind? If that's the case, perhaps you should not have subjected Anne to this abuse."

Lucy's cigarette was down to the filter. She crushed it against the bottom of her shoe until the last stubborn tobacco shreds fell to the floor. She put the remains in a half-full black trash bag. The thought of being exposed as a killer had so preoccupied Lucy's mind that she hadn't considered any other scenario. Marge and Anne's relationship had been overshadowed and forgotten. Did her sister have expectations of being left something? Money? China? A kind word?

"No, that's not what I'm saying." Jack watched Lucy return to her seat. "Lucy, I'll help you find a place to live. With your mother's savings, you should be able to purchase a modest home."

"Did you two ever talk about you becoming a nun?" Anne asked, uncrossing her legs and sitting up straight.

"No." Lucy said. Her wet clothes were cold; goosebumps covered her arms.

"Maybe I should take you home so you can get into some dry clothes." Jack stood and excused himself.

Behind Jack's desk a yellowing set of thick Venetian blinds hung crookedly from the top of the window. Lucy stood to look outside. The sunlight created shadows where the butcher's name and phone number were painted on the glass. She thought that she had expected the worst. Her mother's betrayal. But not in this way.

"Would you want to be a nun?" Anne asked quietly.

"No, Anne. Can you just let it drop?"

"I'm sorry. Maybe you could move away. Or travel. Get out of this place," her sister offered. "Have a whole new life."

Lucy said nothing.

When Jack returned, Brad said, "Are you sure she left Anne nothing. A memento. A family heirloom. Something of her father's perhaps?"

"Why are you surprised, Brad? You knew my mother," Anne said again, patting his hand. "Besides, isn't it tradition? Her parents left her nothing."

A delivery truck barreled down the street, sending vibrations through the building. Lucy could hear pieces of plaster pinging off the glass case.

Chapter Five

On Christmas Eve Lucy sat among the cranberry candles, angel figurines, and jovial Santas that occupied every flat surface in the Garritys' home. Since Marge's death Mrs. Garrity routinely checked on Lucy, and had invited her to their holiday celebrations. Garlands hung from the banister, as well as from window and doorframes. The towels in the bathroom and kitchen were red and green, adorned with snowflakes. Even Mrs. Garrity's evergreen sweater had a manger scene embroidered on it. After her second eggnog, Lucy teased her host that if she stayed too long, she too would be decorated. By a front window, the gigantic Douglas fir loomed, its branches weighed down by lights and handmade ornaments, keepsakes of her sons' and daughters' childhood art projects.

On the couch, Lucy sank deeply into the blue and red floral upholstery, sipping her eggnog, which was spiked with just enough whiskey and too much nutmeg. Mr. Garrity sat next to her, giving quiet commentary about those family members gathered, much like a sportscaster. As Lucy enjoyed the eggnog refill her hostess had anticipated her wanting, Mr. Garrity warned, "That's the beauty of eggnog. On the surface it's a perfectly respectable holiday drink, but it really does get you snockered."

Mrs. Garrity was happiest when her children and grandchildren and great grandchildren were visiting. This time it was one of her daughters and one of her sons, each with a spouse. Their children were in the basement listening to music, playing darts, and drinking soda. Lucy wasn't sure if they were the same ones who visited at Thanksgiving. The Garritys all looked alike to her; even their spouses looked related.

Content with the numbing effect of the drink, Lucy sat quietly next to the Christmas tree as one of the Garrity daughters or daughters-in-law sat at the upright piano. The others gathered around, laughing and talking as they tried to remember the words and sometimes the melodies of Christmas carols. Lucy's father had talked about this family growing up across the street from him in his bachelor days. How they would spill into the street after school to play jump rope or stickball until it was their turn to practice piano. It was hard to hear the one struggling at the piano over their shouting. Now those children were about the same age as Lucy's mother had been, but they were so full of life and happiness.

"Wait 'til they get to 'Silent Night.' It's murder," Mr. Garrity loudly whispered, then laughed.

Mrs. Garrity called across the room to Lucy. If Lucy was not engaged in a conversation for a moment, Mrs. Garrity felt the need to start one. "Oh dear me, Lucy, how could I have forgotten? Jack says he thinks he's found you a house."

"Oh?" Lucy said. The room was loud; she was buzzed. Perhaps she didn't hear correctly.

"Jack says it's not far. St. Catherine's, I think," Mrs. Garrity said.

"Jack says." Mr. Garrity mimicked his wife, then leaned closer to Lucy and quietly said, "Don't get her started on that one. All I hear is 'When's Jack going to settle down?' She's not satisfied that all hers are married off."

"Wouldn't that make for a Merry Christmas?" Mrs. Garrity continued, "Just like something out of *Miracle on 34th Street*. Do you remember that movie? Little Natalie Wood. God rest her soul." She touched her dyed red hair, an attribute that set her apart from the majority of senior ladies in the neighborhood.

"Yes, I remember," Lucy said to her hostess.

"Lucy, why don't you marry him, eh? So I don't have to listen to it." Mr. Garrity winked and raised his glass as if to toast a deal.

"Any word from the Church? Are they putting your mother's house on the market? I just worry about all that riff-raff walking through the house or, God forbid, buying it. You know, we've got to protect this neighborhood. I mean I've got to live here...."

Lucy stopped listening and picked up her eggnog. She excused herself and went into the kitchen. No one else was there. In the center of the table a plastic Santa Claus riding in his reindeer-pulled sleigh called out a "Ho! Ho! Ho!" Red and gold garland was tied to the end of the eggnog ladle. She sat smoking a cigarette, ashing in the reindeer ashtray that must have been made in school by one of the kids, back when kids made ashtrays in school. Perhaps the eggnog was influencing her thought process, but Lucy considered her mother's suggestion of joining the nunnery. A conversation with a nun in high school came to mind. Lucy had said that she wasn't good enough to become a nun, to which Sister John replied, "That's why I became a nun. I knew I needed the extra help." Lucy wasn't sure what kind of problems the nun had faced that led her to take the vows, but she felt certain Sister John hadn't killed her mother.

After cleaning out the ashtray, Lucy downed the rest of her eggnog. She wanted to go home, while it was still her home. She waved good-bye and wished the Garrity family a Merry Christmas.

It was bright outside the Garrity house with Christmas decorations. Blinking lights framed the window. Chained to the railing was an illuminated four-foot-tall plastic candlestick. When Lucy bumped into it, the decoration made a sound like the Big Wheel she had as a kid. Across the street her house seemed dark with just the lamp lit in the window.

Inside, Lucy plugged in the Christmas lights and stretched out on the floor under the tree. The tiny bulbs threw the patterns of the ornaments, garland, and branches across the ceiling. The tree and the manger scene were the only decorations in the house. Marge didn't go in for overdoing it. The tree was fake, its pine needles silver. If she wanted a pine scent, Marge said, she had her all-purpose cleaner. "I don't need to be discovering needles in the furniture and carpet all year-round."

To Lucy, this was Christmas and, on this night, the familiar sight and lack of scent brought her peace. She lay motionless, squinting at the ceiling and the changing patterns the fake branches cast. Still, the thought came back to her. It's happening. It was happening and there wasn't anything she could do to stop it. She was losing her home, her father's home, and being cast out into an unfamiliar neighborhood, among strangers. Maybe she hadn't chosen her life. Maybe it had been established for her, but still it was hers. It was what she knew and what she needed to cling to now. Being alone for the first time in her life was change enough.

For the past two months Lucy had tried to bring the mother she knew back to life. The one who immersed herself in routine, the one who resisted change, the one who came into this house as a newlywed and rarely left. The one who would never give the house away. But this new Marge, the dead one, this untrustworthy Marge, kept resurfacing.

Chapter Six

Smoking wasn't allowed in the Anderson household. It was the primary reason Marge never accepted invitations to visit. When Anne would call about Easter or Christmas, Marge's pat response was, "You know where to find me." Lucy wouldn't have minded the restriction if she felt accommodated in some way. Instead, she was exiled to the cement slab designated as the front porch, without a chair or an ashtray. She had to improvise by filling a plastic cup with a little water. Inside, she'd left Jack with Anne and Brad. The thought of spending Christmas alone with her sister and brother-in-law worried her. Fortunately, Jack was available and even seemed pleased with the idea. Plus, he had a car. Lucy wouldn't be stranded in New Jersey, having to rely on Brad to take her home.

All the condominiums in the development were identical, even down to the shrubbery installed in the short front lawns. Lucy didn't understand why these were any better than row houses. At least at home she could walk to things. Here there were just winding roads with more of the same buildings. The only thing you could walk to was the dumpster, which was situated almost directly in front of Anne's place. Lucy wondered if she got a discount for having to inhale garbage odor. The smell of burning tobacco was an improvement. However, the dumpster did make for easy disposal of the ash-filled cup each time Lucy went out.

When Lucy returned, Anne and Jack were standing in the living room. The ceiling went straight through to the second story. Two windows of the same height flanked the fireplace, and Lucy wondered how they cleaned them. The view was a lawn, vacant of any trees or bushes, and then another set of beige houses. The Christmas tree stood in front of the window to the left. It was real, and Lucy did enjoy the natural smell of it. Anne had decorated it exclusively in pinecones, silver ribbons, and blue lights.

Brad came from the kitchen and stood next to Lucy in the entryway. "It's slow suicide," he said, smiling and nodding toward her cigarette case as though they shared a secret.

Jack was talking about Mrs. Garrity. "Aunt Libby's just praying no blacks will move in. You know those ladies have been Democrats since birth and campaigned for Kennedy, so they think that makes them Liberals. Sure they supported civil rights . . . in the South. That doesn't mean they want them living next door or marrying their daughters."

Brad interrupted. "Well, dinner's almost ready. Why don't we move into the dining room?" The dining room was in an alcove off to the right of the living room. The table was set for four, and Brad sat at the head; Jack sat opposite him. Along the center of the table, three tall red candles stood in a row. Small poinsettia plants were placed on either side of the candles, and ivy was intertwined throughout.

As they sat down across the table from each other, Anne said, "So, Lucy. What are your plans?" There was a slight echo to her voice.

"Excuse me?" Lucy said, positioning herself behind one of the poinsettias.

Brad smiled. "I'll go check on the goose."

Anne sat up straight, granting him a tight-lipped smile as he rested his hand on her shoulder and emptied the last of the wine into her glass. There was a pervasive tension between Anne and Brad that had been apparent from the moment Lucy and Jack had arrived. Lucy couldn't tell if it was her presence or something between them that was causing the problem. It did make her aware of her inability to read her sister.

When Brad was in the kitchen, Anne said, "I know you're still grieving, Lucy. That's only natural, but you have a real opportunity to make some changes."

"Like what?" Lucy said.

"You could move anywhere," she said, straightening a cloth napkin across her lap. It was evergreen with red poinsettias. "You could travel. You could go to school. Get a different job. Anything."

"What makes you think that I want to change? That I don't like my life?" Under the table, Lucy tugged at her forearm hair.

"Mom's gone. There's nothing holding you back now." Anne glanced down at Lucy's arms.

"Why do you think Mom was holding me back?" Lucy took the napkin from her plate and tossed it on her lap.

"I think your sister's only trying to help," Jack said from his end of the table.

"Well, at least think about moving somewhere else," Anne said. "Center City maybe?"

"There's nothing wrong with South Philly, Anne," Jack said.

"Oh come on, Jack. It's a dying neighborhood. There's nothing to do there."

"Well, Lucy's decided to buy a house there," Jack said.

"Where?"

"Not far. St. Catherine's parish," Lucy said. They had talked about it in the car on the way over. Jack had assured her that the house and the neighborhood were very similar to her mother's.

They were quiet and sipped on their wine. Lucy wanted to excuse herself again, despite her fear of getting into a conversation with Brad while getting another makeshift ashtray. Instead, she took her napkin and began polishing the butter knife. In some ways Anne's house was like Marge's. Impeccably clean. Simply furnished. But everything here was brand new. Everything smelt new. Marge maintained her things, the things she'd inherited from Joseph and his father. Her bedroom set was the last furniture purchased.

"I think you should reconsider," Anne said quietly.

"What do you have against South Philly?" Jack said, leaning forward with his hands on the table.

"It's in decline. Who is she going to meet there? What kind of job can she get that's any better than the one she's got?" Anne said.

"There's a strong sense of community and tradition, which some of us appreciate." Jack, suddenly aware of himself, sat back in his chair.

"Jack, I'm sorry, but this isn't about you and your desire to revitalize your neighborhood." Anne was going to continue when Brad entered the room.

"What did I miss?" he said, holding a jug of wine.

"These two are just planning the rest of my life, is all." Lucy said, genuinely pleased that Brad was now in the room.

"Oh," Brad said. Then to Jack, "I thought we'd try the wine you brought with dinner?"

"Sure," said Jack. "See if you like it. One of my clients makes it each Christmas. I know it's not p.c. but he calls it Dego Red."

"I'm up for it," said Brad. "Anne? Lucy?"

Both women nodded, and everyone finished the rest of the wine in their glasses. Brad went around the table with the jug. As he reached in front of Lucy and poured her wine, she looked at her sister.

"I don't understand why I have to do anything. I'm moving. Okay? I'm buying my own house. Isn't that enough change for the time being?"

"I'm just saying that the world's a bigger place than the neighborhood we grew up in. You're young. You're smart. Don't you want to go out into the world? Experiment a little. See things. Meet different kinds of people." Her sister picked up her glass and eyed the red wine.

"Anne, look at where you live. What's so exciting about living here? What's there to do here? What makes your life so much better than mine? That you moved to the next state over?"

"God, you can sound just like her." Anne stood up, placing her napkin on the table. "At least I've gotten that far away. I've been outside the tri-state area. I got an education. Don't you want to meet someone, get married, have children? Excuse me." She went into the kitchen.

"Maybe we should change the subject?" Brad said, holding up a large bowl of salad. "Try some salad." He passed the bowl to Lucy. She filled her plate and handed the bowl to Jack.

Anne returned from the kitchen with a large pepper grinder. "Pepper, anyone?" The four sat quietly chewing their salad. Brad sipped the wine and declared it not bad at all.

"Lucy, does this mean you've decided not to become a nun?" Anne chortled in what seemed like an effort to lighten the mood.

"Why would you think I'd become a nun?" Lucy tried to sound calm.

"I don't know," she said. "I haven't really spent any time with you since you were in high school but you seemed pretty religious then."

"What? Because I went to church on Sunday?" Lucy couldn't be sure why she felt so defensive. Being a nun was a perfectly honorable calling, but she found the concept patronizing coming from her sister.

"That's religious to me. Besides it was more than that. You know what I mean."

Lucy just stared at her.

Anne continued, "I'm sorry if I offended you. I'm sure you've changed a lot. I know I'm not the same person."

"I was never nun material." Lucy said.

Brad interrupted, "Anyone need anything while I'm up?" All three mumbled that they didn't.

The goose was an Anderson family tradition. Over dinner, Jack continued to make pleasant conversation, mostly with Brad. He avoided the topic of Lucy's new home. Brad talked about work, then about Christmas when he was a child. Anne showed little interest in his stories, which was unlike her. In the past, she'd been attentive and had had only praise for her husband. Lucy wondered if that had been for Marge's benefit or if something else had changed.

"You have a lovely home," Jack said to Brad. "How long have you lived here?"

"About eight years now," Brad said, as he poured himself more wine from the jug. "We picked the plot back when it was just a dirt field. That way we could choose some of the unique features, such as the fireplace, the ceiling fans, the skylights, and what color carpet we wanted throughout. It's worked out well for us. We got the exact home we wanted."

After dinner they sat in the living room drinking coffee, eating chocolate mousse, and exchanging gifts. Anne gave Lucy a self-help book for daughters who have lost their mothers. Lucy smiled and thanked her. Even if Lucy considered reading that type of book, this one didn't apply to her. She hadn't lost her mother, hadn't misplaced her, she'd killed her. Did they have a book for that? Each Christmas, Lucy felt that Anne gave her a gift that was meant to improve her. This year, Lucy tried to respond in kind. In addition to the traditional wool scarf and mittens, she gave her a book on how to get rid of every kind of stain.

Outside on the porch, it was dark. Lucy could see the Christmas lights in the other houses. She wondered if Anne's neighbors were true believers. Marge once said, or maybe she said it more than once, "On Saint Patrick's Day, everybody thinks they're Irish. It's an excuse to get drunk. The same goes for Christmas. Suddenly, everybody's a Jesus-lover for the gifts." Despite the tension at times, the night had turned out okay. It was better than spending Christmas alone. It was even a little better than spending it with the Garritys; there were so many of them, it made her feel lonelier.

Anne came out, her cardigan pulled close around her. "It's cold out here," Anne said.

Lucy remained silent, expecting Anne to lecture her on the evils of smoking. She took a deep drag.

Jack came out carrying Lucy's coat, followed by Brad. The four said their Merry Christmases and thank yous, then parted. Lucy made her final ashtray deposit in the dumpster on the way to Jack's car.

As they sat in the car letting it warm up, Jack handed Lucy a bottle of antacid.

"Sometimes I can't believe I'm related to her. We're so different," Lucy said. Then she dropped two tablets in her mouth. The crunching sound as she chewed blocked out the sound of the car engine. She watched Jack's jaw working, his throat swallowing. His hands rested on the top of the steering wheel and he seemed to be considering his opposable thumbs.

"Lucy, answer me honestly here, okay?" he said.

"Okay." Lucy swallowed.

"Do you want to stay in South Philly or did I just assume that?" His hands were still on the steering wheel, but he was looking directly at her.

"Yes. I want to stay there," Lucy put her hands under her behind. The car was still cold. "Jack, I don't want to move at all. I want to stay in my house. You know that."

"I know. But you have to move. You have no choice about that. You do have a choice about where you want to move."

"It's fine."

Jack pulled out of the driveway and after a few attempts, found his way out of the development and onto the highway. As they traveled across the bridge, Lucy revisited the conversation with her sister and became irritated. Why was her sister suddenly so concerned with how she lived her life? Was it because their mother was dead? Had the dynamic changed just because Marge wasn't in the room? Or did Anne feel responsible for her little sister's happiness? Neither of them had a mother or a father anymore. What were they to each other now?

Chapter Seven

Lucy pulled the Tuesday index card from her mother's recipe box; cleaning all glass surfaces topped the list. Routine, she believed, kept her from unraveling. By performing these daily chores, she hoped she would eventually catch, like a chain in the teeth of a gear, and be propelled forward through life. But as she dutifully completed these tasks in the order dictated, she would ruminate over her mother's selfishness and secrecy. If she couldn't trust her own mother to love her and to look out for her, especially when Lucy had taken care of her, then what kind of person did that make Lucy? If her own mother didn't love her?

The screen door squeaked open and she heard Mrs. Garrity calling, "Hello, Lucy. Are you up?"

"In here."

"What are you doing?" Mrs. Garrity came into the kitchen.

"Having breakfast," Lucy said, and then lit a cigarette. She suspected that Mrs. Garrity's spontaneous visit was about the pink-and-white ceramic mixing bowls Marge left her in the will. Lucy's intention was to gather the things Marge had left the neighbors after she finished her chores for the day. The thought of this activity raised her ire too; her mother had been so thoughtful toward the old ladies, so specific in what they would want.

Mrs. Garrity helped herself to a cup of coffee and sat down. "Have you forgotten you've gotta be out of here in two days?"

"No," Lucy said. The Church planned to use the house for semiretired

priests. On Thursday, contractors were scheduled to make the house handi-
cap accessible. With Jack's help, she'd reluctantly bought the house in St.
Catherine's parish, which was about ten blocks away in a different neighborhood. It had two major things going for it — it was available, and Lucy
could afford it.

As Lucy cleaned the ashtray, there was a knock at the door. There she
found Mrs. Carson leading a slow procession of three women making their
way to her stoop. The word was out, Lucy guessed, that she was leaving
and they were coming to claim their Marge memorabilia. As the neighbors
entered the living room, they sighed in relief that everything wasn't in boxes,
and then expressions of confusion spread from one to the next.

"Deary, I thought I heard you were moving?"

"Did Mrs. Garrity get her dates mixed up?"

Lucy simply held the door open until the last of the fortune seekers arrived.

"Mrs. Garrity's in the kitchen," Lucy directed them.

"Oh, is she here?"

"Let me find my mother's list."

"Oh, we were just coming to wish you well." They murmured as they
swayed awkwardly, clasping their hands or adjusting their eyeglasses.

Mrs. Garrity called from the kitchen, "Come on in, girls. I just put on a
fresh pot."

*   *   *

The list was in an envelope on top of Lucy's bureau, which stood in an
alcove between two closets. Above it hung a matching mirror, waiting to
be cleaned. As a child, Lucy often thought the alcove would be the perfect
place for the Blessed Mother to appear to her. Lucy would lie in bed staring
at the spot, waiting, envisioning that image of Mary, and wondering if Mary
appeared, would she be called Our Lady of South Philadelphia? Would
Lucy automatically be made a saint? Would she be on the news? But the
Virgin Mary never appeared, and part of Lucy was grateful. Waking up to
a religious vision would have been, in fact, scary. The new house didn't have
an alcove in the back bedroom, Lucy's room. So many things were wrong
with the new place.

Lucy could hear the whispering in the kitchen below her. Since half of
the women were hard of hearing, it came out as loud hissing. They were
older than her mother was. They must have been in their thirties and forties
when Marge moved in as a teenage bride. Why had her mother befriended
them when there were other young mothers in the neighborhood?

To Lucy's relief, each of the ladies in the kitchen was left something. The
list contained items that Lucy could part with easily — the mixing bowls,

an English teapot (never used), and crystal salt and pepper shakers. One dispersed too much and the other too little.

In the kitchen, the ladies were more relaxed now, with their respective gifts in front of them. Marge must have told each of them what to expect. They made room for Lucy at the table, and she resumed her breakfast, lighting a cigarette. Mrs. Carson sat contentedly with the English teapot nestled on her ample thighs. The desire to suffocate them all filled Lucy; Marge had been so thoughtful with them and not with her own daughters. They slurped their coffee with an occasional glance toward Mrs. Garrity, who seemed to be holding them there somehow.

Finally she spoke. "I called Jack. He's renting a van and should be here in a little while."

"I can call a moving company," Lucy said.

"I don't think you'd be able to get one on such short notice. That's not the way it works." Mrs. Garrity always spoke with authority, no matter what the topic.

After tapping her cigarette on the edge of the ashtray, Lucy carefully pulled on individual forearm hairs with the same hand. Ashes fell on her arm; she blew them away, avoiding eye contact with her guests. She compared the brown cigarette to the pigment of her arm. They had gotten their stuff; they should have gone. Once she moved, they'd forget about her until one of them dropped dead and turned up at the funeral home. She swore, as she successfully yanked out one hair and rewarded herself with a deep drag on the cigarette, that she would not pick the wilting flowers from that one's flower arrangements at the end of the evening; she wouldn't vacuum the tissue residue from the carpet. Most definitely, she would hold back on saying even the obligatory, "She was a good woman."

"And we're all volunteering to help you pack. Isn't that right, girls?" Mrs. Garrity continued. There was no response, with the exception of some shuffling among the contingency. Not everyone seemed happy with this statement.

"Well, today's my day to make lasagna. You know how Bill loves his lasagna," one said as she stood.

"I've got my shopping," another followed the first, waving farewell.

Only Mrs. Carson was left, sitting silently, rubbing the teapot as if a genie was going to appear and give her a legitimate excuse. Mrs. Garrity had clamped her arm as the other two quickly parted with their loot in hand.

"I'll be fine." Lucy held her mouth shut tightly. Opening and closing her mouth to smoke felt like a production, like a snake unhinging its jaw. The coffee pot hissed. Mrs. Carson stirred her half-full coffee cup until Mrs. Garrity released her. At that point, she stood up, stating that she had laundry to hang but would be back. The lid of the teapot clattered as she stumbled out. Lucy was feeling Marge-like. When the women tried to recreate this scene for whoever was on the other end of the phone line later that day, it would be difficult for them to describe the tension and why they were nervous, for Lucy really hadn't done or said anything extraordinary. Although she might have been curt, she was polite.

"Did you know my mother gave the house away?" Lucy said to the only remaining one.

"Of course. Your mother told me everything," Mrs. Garrity said. The sun was on the back of her head and her hair looked thin and slightly maroon. She held a yellow mug with both hands. The mugs matched the walls. They were supposed to be cheery, but Lucy heard once that painting your walls yellow was a sign of depression.

"Did you try to talk her out of it?"

"Your mother was devoted to the Church, like most converts. Although, Lord knows, she held on to some of her Protestant ways. Her work ethic for one and, of course, she stopped at two." Mrs. Garrity sipped her coffee. "Never even tried for a boy to have a priest in the family — although she held out hope that you might join the convent someday. Of course, the Church appealed to your mother's love of ritual. Everything was a ritual with her, everyday. Anyway, maybe she thought donating the house to the Church would put her that much closer to heaven."

"Did you tell her they don't do indulgences anymore?" Lucy didn't remember her mother being a convert. One more thing the neighbor knew that Marge's own children didn't. Lucy chose not to mention this to Mrs. Garrity. She considered that this may have been the cause of her mother's split with her family, and not the fact that her father was Italian. Now she wished she'd pressed her mother for more information about her family. Now that she was an orphan, she wanted family.

"What's done is done. For the love of God, you've got your whole life ahead of you."

What's done is done, Lucy thought, my mother is dead. Had she told Mrs. Garrity about those plans?

*　　*　　*

Marge had been a packrat, but not the typical packrat. While it was true she rarely threw anything away — each week's trash barely filled half a grocery bag — she was organized. Each saved item was immediately placed with its kind in its proper place, be it a drawer, accordion file, or labeled carton in the basement. This control over the household inventory made the job of packing up the house an easier task.

In the basement, along with the filing cabinets of financial papers organized by year, Marge had squirreled away enough flattened cardboard boxes, mailing tape, and bubble wrap to meet all the needs of the move. When Jack arrived, he found Lucy assembling boxes. The ceiling was low, and even though he had enough room, Jack kept his head bent, giving him a reverent posture.

"Is this okay with you?" he said. "I didn't realize you hadn't lined up movers."

"It's fine. You're here. Your aunt's probably packed the whole kitchen by now." Lucy continued to tape the bottom of a box.

"It'll be good to get it over with. Besides, you're already paying the mortgage at the new place." Jack folded a box.

"I guess everyone thinks I should be running from this place, but it's my home. I still can't believe she did this." She handed him the tape and scissors.

"I'm sorry."

"I lived my whole life with her. Everyday. And I don't know anything about her. Or why she did the things she did. How is that possible?" Lucy tossed the box behind her with the other assembled boxes. "And this is the person in my life who I knew best. What does that say about me?"

Jack stood, hands full, wanting to comfort her and looking for a place to put everything down. But he missed his opportunity to embrace her; she pulled the next flattened box.

"Don't do that to yourself," he said. "You have to admit your mother was kind of a prickly character. She kept you at a distance. It's nothing you did."

"I don't know."

"You loved her. You trusted her. You were a good daughter," Jack said.

The boxes were piling up around Lucy, so Jack gathered as many as he could carry and took them upstairs.

The three of them worked quietly throughout the day. Despite her reluctance to move, Lucy found working with them comforting. Their progress was swift. Jack's presence, as usual, had a calming effect. He seemed to anticipate where she was going or what she needed, always ready with tape, scissors, a hammer, a screwdriver, or a stepstool.

Jack recruited a few of the older neighborhood kids returning home from school to help carry the heavy furniture and boxes. After they had loaded Lucy's bedroom furniture and boxes into the van, Jack asked her where they should go in the new house.

"In the back bedroom." She sat outside on the stoop, taking a cigarette break. Across the street, St. Valentine's decorations adorned the windows.

"But wouldn't you like to take the front bedroom?"

"For now, just put everything where it was here," she said. Her plan had been to have no plan. Her plan was to wish the whole thing away.

"Young man," Mrs. Garrity called out from one of the upstairs windows. "Why are you so concerned with where she sleeps? Do as she asks."

Mrs. Garrity had volunteered to pack Marge's room. She was surprised to discover that everything of Marge's remained untouched, and she insisted that they pack up her clothes and give them away to St. Vincent's.

"There's no reason to move this stuff to the new house. You're not using it." Mrs. Garrity held out a bunch of worn housedresses. Marge always dressed about thirty years older than she was.

"Just pack them."

"Lucy, you need to do this at some point. Why not now?"

"Not today," Lucy said.

Throughout the afternoon, Jack made trips back and forth between the houses, following Lucy's instructions. The boxes were put in the rooms designated in marker on their tops. The furniture was put in as close proximity to the original locations as possible. They continued packing and hauling throughout the day, stopping only to eat. By day's end, the house was empty. They'd packed everything from the shades and curtains to the remainder of the roll of toilet paper. So Lucy had no choice but to sleep at the other house. Mrs. Garrity hugged Lucy goodbye and took her ceramic bowls home. Jack waited in the van with the last of the boxes to go to the new house.

The streetlamp cast a dim light in the living room. Lucy could see the outlines of the pictures — pictures of her parents' wedding, Lucy's and Anne's First Communions, Pope John Paul II, and John F. Kennedy — that had hung on the wall. She walked slowly through the first floor with her jewelry box held tightly in her arm. Stopping, she swayed and heard the familiar squeaking of the floorboards beneath her feet. During the past few months, there had been moments when Lucy let herself believe that her mother, the one she trusted, was still alive. While watching game shows and enjoying an after-dinner smoke, she would catch a glimpse of her mother next to her or hear her mother's voice call a contestant, "Idiot." Late at night, she'd hear her mother walking around upstairs. In the morning she'd wake up certain she smelled coffee brewing.

In the middle of the dining room Lucy paused. It smelt of pine cleaner and garlic and mothballs and cigarette smoke. It smelt of her mother. This was where she came to say goodbye, again. Lucy wondered if this would be the end, if this was where their murderous secret died. In a new house, would she be able to forget? In a new parish would she finally be able to confess?

She hugged the jewelry box. To the index cards with her mother's murder instructions, she'd added her mother's holy card, her last cigarette box, and the copies of her obituary. She kept collecting these things. The dining room walls seemed to breathe and with each inhalation they drained Lucy of her energy, with each exhalation they filled her with memories. Year after year these walls had witnessed a family's holiday celebrations, but in the end what they saw was a woman dying and a woman killing.

"Goodbye, Mom." Lucy turned to leave, but returned to the dining room window and opened it.

* * *

The first night at the new house, Lucy slept on the couch beneath a large mirror made up of nine gold-flecked panels, which were mounted onto the living room wall. She dreamt again that she was being suffocated. She couldn't breathe, but this time she decided not to fight it. Someone had told her once that if you dreamt that you were falling, maybe down a well or into a canyon, and you hit the bottom, that you really died, not only in your dream but also in real life. Lucy wondered if it was the same with suffocating. Then she woke up.

The morning sun came through the naked front window and woke her to the empty house full of boxes. It seemed as if she woke to another dream. The type of dream where you're walking through a house, a house that isn't where you grew up, but nevertheless, in the dream you recognize that that is exactly what it is representing. The house Lucy walked through had an *Alice-in-Wonderland* feel. The stairs and the front door were on the opposite side of the house from the way they were at her mother's; both should have been on the right, not the left. Here the furniture was oversized, as if it had grown overnight. And while all her things were clean, there was an unknown dust, an unfamiliar residue in the air, which she noticed as she watched her reflection in the large speckled mirror that hung over the couch.

Chapter Eight

Through the kitchen window, Lucy saw the remnants of a garden in the backyard as she filled the bucket with hot water. When she first saw it, her reaction was to have the yard cemented up, as it was at the old house. Her mother couldn't stand the idea of all that dirt and those bugs right outside the door. Houseplants were completely out of the question. On the occasions when her father brought home roses for his wife, Marge would intercept him on the stoop to closely inspect them for any bugs before he was permitted to bring them in the house. Lucy didn't have money to have concrete poured, so the dirt would have to stay.

The garden was one of the many things that set Lucy off kilter. Her new life was confusing. She didn't know anyone in the neighborhood. No matter how hard she concentrated, she couldn't remember how the corner grocery was organized. It took all her energy to feed herself three square meals a day and make her way through the unfamiliar streets to work a few times a week. As she unpacked, she continued to assemble everything as it had always been. How else to do it?

The scrub brush floated on top of the water in the bucket, surrounded by walls of bubbles. She turned off the water and let the bubbles settle. The kitchen was a mossy green, the counter, a dingy beige that resembled a stale kaiser roll in texture and color. The dish rack was too tall to fit under the cabinet to the right of the sink, so Lucy had to put it on the left. Since there wasn't as much cabinet space as in Marge's kitchen, baking pans and cutting boards sat on the dining room table. She wasn't sure what would become of them. But she'd hung the white curtains with the brown-and-gold embroidery, and the metal spice rack. Her mother's recipe box was wider than the windowsill, but Lucy put it in its proper place anyway.

It had been almost a month since Lucy moved, and in that time she hadn't been able to attend to the daily chores properly. This was the first Saturday she was scrubbing the front stoop. The morning was freakishly warm for March. There were still stains on the steps and sidewalk from salt sprinkled down earlier in the week. She surveyed the street. To the uninitiated eye, the block looked like her old block with its two-story, brick-front row homes, narrow sidewalks, and spotting of trees. But these houses weren't the backdrop of her childhood. This wasn't the street on which her father played baseball with the neighborhood kids. These weren't her neighbors.

A few kids in Flyers T-shirts played street hockey, and a handful of old men smoked cigars outside the candy store on the corner. Some of the houses shared stoops with their neighbors, but Lucy's stood alone. As she knelt on the sidewalk and began cleaning the top step, she felt vulnerable, as if someone were watching her. This wasn't the first time she'd felt this since she moved into the house. Every time she'd banged a nail into a wall to hang a picture or a mirror, her rapping was mimicked. A psychic she saw on a talk show years ago said that that was a sign of haunting. One should never respond in kind; it was an invitation to possession by the devil. She focused on the brush and the sensation it sent up her arm as she dragged it back and forth, then dunked it into the hot, sudsy water. The problem with truly cleaning something, with paying attention to it, caring for it, is that every flaw becomes known. The worn marble step was loose and a little crooked. She tried to push it into place, but she only made it wobblier.

Suddenly the front doors of the houses on either side of hers opened simultaneously and two elderly women emerged, one from each house, with tattered lawn chairs under their arms. There was a faint smell of mothballs. Both wore housedresses with small floral patterns whose colors had faded from so many washings. They might have been twins. Except for the eternally pregnant pouch each of them carried, they were relatively thin. Their hair was short and gray.

The women moved in synchronicity as they held onto their wrought-iron railings and used the metal frames of their chairs as canes. Clicking sounds emanated from their hip joints, punctuating their slow progress. They brought their chairs to the edge of their houses so that they were as close to each other, as close to Lucy, as possible without being on her property. They sat facing the street.

Lucy plunged the brush into the water and looked to the woman on her right with a faint smile. No response. Then she turned to the other — the same. No response. They didn't acknowledge Lucy and they didn't look at each other, they just stared straight ahead at the street. For a moment Lucy thought they'd come out to watch the boys play or, from the grumpy expressions on their faces, to yell at them. She retrieved her brush and scrubbed the lower step.

"Do you have bleach in there?" The one on the right finally broke the silence.

"We use bleach. You hafta use bleach to get them white," the one on the left chimed in.

"Yes," Lucy lied.

"Doesn't smell like bleach. You gotta use bleach." Again from the right.

"I am," Lucy reiterated. She stood up to get fresh water to rinse the steps.

"You're not done?" a voice said. Lucy couldn't be sure from which direction it came.

"Well, I have to rinse them yet," Lucy said, looking at the steps.

"You didn't do a good job on this side," from the right.

"Or this side. You can't just do the tops, you gotta do the sides," from the left.

Lucy bent and surveyed the sides. Under such unwelcome scrutiny, she'd forgotten to clean them. Hoping to placate the two women, she knelt again and scrubbed one side and then the other. After each, she looked to the corresponding woman for a nod of approval.

"She kept her steps so clean. Never a smudge," the woman on the right said loudly as she pulled herself up in her chair and held her chin high. "Scrubbed them white with bleach the morning she died. No one was gonna see her steps filthy, 'specially on the day she died."

"She was a good woman." The one on the left bowed her head and blessed herself. Then she looked at Lucy and said, "Those are our sister's steps."

Lucy went into the kitchen and dumped the bucket, all the while muttering to herself, "Their sister's steps. They're mine and I'll clean them the way my mother would. Who are they to tell me how to clean?" She grew impatient waiting for the bucket to fill up, and cut off the water before the bucket was three-quarters full. The water slopped as she charged through the house to the door. The screen door slammed into the railing as she tossed the water on the steps. She closed the storm door and locked it. Their voices carried in through the windows.

"She would have come out and swept the curb."

"Nothing like doing half the job."

"Look at those suds just sitting there. And I still don't smell no bleach."

"Kinda late in the day to be doing it anyway."

"You're right. The light's all wrong."

"Some people's children!"

Lucy walked into the kitchen. How long could they go on discussing the steps? For the first time, she truly missed the old women in her neighborhood. At least their talk was interesting. Sisters, some sisters, are the worst. They can have the same conversation over and over again. They can talk a subject to death.

There was a knock at the door, a persistent knock. Finally, Lucy swung open the door, prepared to defend her cleaning integrity, and discovered a young woman standing in front of her. "Oh," Lucy said.

"Hi, I'm Colleen. Your neighbor from across the street. You got coffee?" In her hands, she held a store-bought box of raspberry pastry. Half of it was missing.

Lucy pushed open the screen door.

Colleen slipped in, calling over her shoulder to the women, "Sorry there ain't enough for you." She laughed a somewhat alarming laugh, a nasal snort.

Lucy let her pass and promptly closed the door as though a cat was about to make its escape. They stood for a moment in the living room. Lucy could still hear the women outside. "Lavella water. That was the best for cleaning steps."

While Colleen studied the room, Lucy stared at Colleen. Her new neighbor was about her age, maybe a few years younger. Her strawberry-blond hair was teased about two inches off her head. Colleen walked over to get a better view of the pictures on the wall, but lost interest quickly. Lucy noticed how very thin she was. She barely had a figure and her tight, cropped jeans and spaghetti-strap T-shirt revealed the specifics of her bone placement. Her small eyes were outlined in dark blue eyeliner.

Colleen opened her mouth and began what would be sustained talk for the next hour and a half. "I thought you lived alone. Do you live with your folks?" Lucy shook her head. "God this place is crazy. Like a time warp or something. Is it intentional? 'Cause I think you gotta update your look here, sister." Lucy walked into the kitchen and Colleen followed. "Holy shit, we used to have those curtains when I was a kid." Colleen sat down at the table, opened the cake box, and sliced herself a piece while Lucy poured coffee. "So I see you met the Delvecchio sisters. Thank God one is dead. One down, two to go. Lina, Gina, and Dina ruled the block for decades. I don't even know their married names. They lived right next to each other. Can you imagine their poor husbands? I wouldn't even have done that to my ex, the asshole. I think you got Lina's, the dead one's, house. Really, I'm not usually the neighborly type, but I saw them torturing you and couldn't not do something. Besides, there ain't that many young people around here. I wouldn't be here, except for the asshole."

Occasionally Lucy got in a yes, no, or uh-huh, but she didn't mind Colleen dominating the conversation. It had been a long time since anyone wanted to talk to her. It had been a long time since she had someone her own age to talk to. Lucy tried to figure out her guest. Colleen looked like she had been in the cool crowd in high school, definitely someone who wouldn't have seen quiet, unassuming Lucy scurrying from class to class. Colleen strove to be noticed, while Lucy strove to be undetected. Time outside of school sometimes made people more open-minded, usually out of need. Colleen was a good talker and Lucy had had years of practice at being a listener. That morning they smoked Lucy's cigarettes and Lucy learned all about Colleen, what grade school and high school she went to, her early and brief marriage, her daughter Tiffany, and her ex-husband, the asshole. And Colleen learned very little about Lucy. For Lucy this was fine. The only thing interesting she'd ever done in her life she couldn't talk about.

Chapter Nine

Colleen became a regular at Lucy's kitchen table, coming by most weekday mornings after dropping Tiffany off at school. Once a week, Lucy would take Colleen shopping at the Italian Market. Mostly though, they drank coffee, smoked cigarettes, and talked about television shows and celebrities. When Colleen heard that St. Catherine of Alexandra Church, Lucy's new parish, was hosting a Catholic singles dance, she decided to give Lucy a makeover. Lucy wasn't too surprised; makeovers were Colleen's favorite part of the morning talk shows. Also, Colleen worked at a neighborhood hair salon, ringing up customers and occasionally washing hair. The dance would be Lucy's unofficial coming-out party, Colleen said. After that, Lucy would be ready to hit the clubs on Delaware Avenue.

Colleen arrived at her house early Saturday morning and woke Lucy, who was sleeping in, having decided to cross stoop cleaning off that day's index card.

"What time is it?" Lucy grunted, after stumbling out of bed. She never would have agreed to this makeover if she knew it would be an all-day process.

"It's eight. We've got a lot of work to do." Despite the hour, Colleen was completely put together. Her lipstick matched the pink of her T-shirt. Her eyeliner was drawn in perfect lines. Meanwhile, Lucy stood half-asleep and unwashed in a sleeveless nightgown she'd had since high school.

"You look like Laura Ingalls in that thing," Colleen said, pulling at the worn cotton.

"Good morning, Miss Pescitelli," a groggy Tiffany said in a singsong fashion before climbing onto the couch. She clutched her favorite stuffed animal, a purple bear that was once Colleen's, and tried to find a comfortable position for her curler-covered head on the plastic slipcover.

Colleen put on the TV, then sat next to Tiffany and began unrolling the curlers.

"I left a note on our door telling her father that we'd be here. Hope that's okay. He has her for the day," said Colleen.

"Mom, the picture's all zigzaggy."

Lucy played with the rabbit ears until the big-headed cartoons came in clearer. She was glad to know that Colleen didn't refer to her ex as "the asshole" when talking to her daughter.

"Daddy should be here in a little bit. We'll be in the kitchen," Colleen said when she was done brushing out Tiffany's hair.

"Sit," Colleen said, as she pulled a chair away from the kitchen table and faced it toward the window. From the depths of a brown paper bag, she produced an instant camera. "I hope you don't mind. I thought it would be fun to have before- and after-pictures." She positioned Lucy's chin before snapping the first picture.

Lucy flinched. She tried to stand, but Colleen easily pushed her back into the chair. "Colleen. Coffee," she cried.

"Oh, all right. I'll have some too. I can get this started while it brews." Colleen snapped a quick picture of Lucy's profile. From the bag she pulled a clay pot filled with something called Stardust, and a variety of small, flat plastic knives. She filled a saucepan with water and placed the clay pot inside.

"Do you torture all your friends this way?" Lucy said, as she smoked her morning cigarette and stared at the coffee dripping into the pot. Even in her morning haze, Lucy realized that Colleen didn't talk about her other friends. Maybe she had scared them all away. Or maybe, she didn't talk about them because Lucy never mentioned having other friends.

"I'll have you know, this is the latest in hair removal technology from the Home Shopping Network."

"Uh-huh," said Lucy.

"So NASA develops this formula as an adhesive for the tiles on the outside of the Space Shuttle," Colleen continued as she stirred the thick blue wax with a plastic knife. "But it burns off when they re-enter the earth's atmosphere. Tiles go flying. One of the astronauts brings a jar of it home as a souvenir, and his daughter decides to smear it all over Stardust, the family cat. Cat must have been half dead not to notice. Anyway, the astronaut discovers the cat, and pulls the gunk off. Stardust's hair comes off with it. The cat feels no pain."

"You know, I've killed before," Lucy said.

"But you really shouldn't let children play with it," Colleen said, unaffected by Lucy's threat. "Stardust is toxic if ingested."

The water came to a boil. Colleen placed the pot on the counter and stirred the waxy substance until she wrestled a small amount away. It was a fluorescent blue. "Let's start with an arm. Just in case you have some sort of reaction," she said, taking Lucy's left arm.

Lucy pulled away.

"Here kitty, kitty," Colleen laughed, "Don't worry, it's hypoallergenic."

The blue smeared across her forearm. The warmth felt nice. Maybe it wouldn't be too bad, Lucy considered, as she sipped her coffee and took a drag from her cigarette. Once, after being taunted on the playground with serenades of "George of the Jungle," she'd stolen her father's razor and, unaware of the nuances of shaving, dry-shaved her forearms. She was amazed at how quickly the hair came off, but she immediately developed a rash, which forced her to wear long sleeves for a few days, even to bed.

Lucy held her breath as Colleen grabbed the end of the blue smear and ripped it off her arm.

"Ow!" Smoke escaped her mouth.

"I hope we have enough for your bikini lines. You never know, you might get lucky tonight," Colleen chortled.

"Colleen!" Lucy looked over her shoulder toward the living room.

"What? How long's it been?"

Lucy didn't reply; she'd always assumed that her virginity was noticeable even to the casual passerby.

"Lucy?"

Her cigarette had burned out. She grabbed another one from her pack and lit it without cleaning the ashtray.

"Oh ... my ... God." Colleen gasped between each word, and tried to establish eye contact. "Oh my God. Really?"

Lucy rolled the tip of her cigarette along the rim of the ashtray, watching the ashes fall into the pit. "Shut up."

"Oh my God," Colleen said, trying to stifle a snort.

"Stop saying that."

"Do we need to have a talk, young lady?"

"I don't want to talk about this."

Colleen continued to spread Stardust on Lucy's arms and rip it off, even though at times her body shook from holding back the laughter. Meanwhile, Lucy concentrated on the pain. It became clear that Lucy wasn't suffering from any immediate reaction to the formula, so Colleen smeared a thick slab of it on Lucy's sideburn. As she ripped the wax off, there was a knock at the door. Lucy's face stung.

"Tiffany, that's your father. Get your backpack," Colleen shouted, still holding the drooping wax in her hand. She tossed it back into the clay pot and patted Lucy on the shoulder. "Be right back."

She could hear Colleen saying goodbye to Tiffany, instructing her to be good. She couldn't hear any conversation between Colleen and her ex. He may have been waiting in the car. When she returned, she continued in silence yanking at Lucy's skin. Lucy's face was numb by the time Colleen had extracted all hair deemed extraneous.

"I need a break. Why don't I run and get some hoagies down the street? You want to split an American or Italian?" said Colleen.

"American, with oil," said Lucy, rubbing her cheeks.

"And you can take care of that bikini line. We can do your legs after lunch. I'll need to heat up more Stardust for them."

Lucy surveyed the pot of Stardust and the plastic knife.

"Unless you want me to do it?" said Colleen. "I'm fine with that."

"No, I'll do it," Lucy said as she gathered the equipment.

"Where you going?"

"The bathroom. Alone." All that hair. In the kitchen. Even though it was captured in blue wax, Lucy thought, Marge would have been repulsed by the idea of it.

As Lucy ascended the living room stairs, she caught a glimpse of herself in the gold flecks and foggy glass of the mirror that hung on the opposite wall. It was nearly the length of the couch. Each time she saw herself in it, she felt caught in a flashback sequence from a seventies movie. Maybe in this one, she was reminiscing about her prom night.

Two fluorescent bulbs lit either side of the bathroom mirror. Lucy missed the natural light from the skylight in the old bathroom. Her skin looked freshly peeled and its tone resembled that of the peach tile that covered most of the walls. Colleen had pulled her hair back in a taut ponytail. Bits of blue clung to her face and neck and arms. She splashed cold water from the faucet on her face again and again until she could feel the sensation of its coolness against her skin. Then she patted her face with a soft terry cloth towel. When she let her hand drop from her face, she was startled that the figure in the mirror followed her actions. Normally, she didn't examine herself this closely. As she ran her hand over her cheek, her skin was so cool and smooth, it reminded her of when she'd touched her mother's dead face. Was Marge watching? Thoughts of her mother always made her feel breathless.

Tonight she would go to St. Catherine's for the first time and it was for a singles' dance, not confession. She'd walked past the church many times now, even imagined herself kneeling in the cool darkness of the confessional, inhaling the scent of lingering incense. What would she say? "Father, I, uh, sorta suffocated my mother to death, but she wanted me to. She was in a lot of pain. She made me, really. You had to know her." But Lucy knew it was her sin. She couldn't place the blame on her dead mother who had already faced her judgment. What would the priest say?

"You need help in there?" Colleen called, trying the door.

"No, I'll be down in a minute." Lucy stirred the Stardust.

"I saw your friend getting lunch."

"Who?" Lucy spread the formula on her bikini line, trying not to be distracted by Colleen's yammering.

"Jack Kelleher. Hey, does he have a girlfriend?"

"No. They broke up awhile ago, I think," Lucy said as she tried to grasp the end of the blue strip.

"Interesting. Maybe you could hook up with him? Get it over with," Colleen said.

"Ow!" Lucy yelled as she ripped it off.

Colleen continued without missing a beat. "I'd do him myself, but he's got that nice-guy thing going on. I go for the bad boys."

Lucy rubbed her skin, tears running down her face. "Could you give me a few minutes alone?"

"Didn't you say he helped you find this house? A house in his neighborhood? And he helped you move?"

"Yeah," Lucy said, as she stared at her crotch.

"Well, duh, even nice guys are nice for a reason."

"Colleen, he's like a brother. Okay?"

"Uh-huh. Well, lunch is here." Colleen rumbled down the steps.

*   *   *

Lucy didn't own a dress. Once Colleen recovered from this news, they set out for a dress shop on Passyunk Avenue. Terry, the owner, was a customer at Colleen's hair salon. She asked Lucy to turn around slowly while she eyed her build. She asked for her bra size and shoe size, and sent her to the dressing room with Colleen. Ten minutes later, Terry returned with an armful of dresses, two boxes of shoes, and underwear. Lucy held up the padded bra and tiny panties in dismay. One seemed to work too hard, the other not at all.

Terry noted her expression. "If you want to look good you have to start from the bottom up," she said as she left the room.

Lucy insisted that Colleen look away while she tried on the bra and matching thong underwear. The round platform in the dressing room was surrounded by a three-panel mirror. The underwear was a matching set in lavender. Lucy's skin appeared greenish under the buzzing overhead lights. Turning from right to left, she could see her body in multiples from every angle. She held in her tummy. The elastic waistband of her old underwear had left a line just above her navel that encircled her midriff. Ragged lines traveled down her sides where the seams had been. Her butt was meant to be covered. She felt more than naked; she felt skinned.

In sixth grade, overnight, Lucy developed breasts. Her classmates, particularly the boys, were confused. They had a solid repertoire of ridicule about her body hair. Then the sudden introduction of breasts: was this girl a slut because she had breasts, or a boy because of all the hair? Finally, they decided to call her a dyke. That day she ran home from school and found her mother scouring the oven.

When she asked her mother what it meant, Marge pulled her head out of the oven and said, "Where did you hear that, young lady?"

"Kids at school."

"Well, you'd better confess it." Her voice echoed as she retreated back into the oven.

"But I didn't do anything. I don't even know what it means. What do I tell Father?"

Without looking at her daughter, Marge said, "Just say impure thoughts." A gloved hand emerged and shooed Lucy away.

The quick pace of dressing and undressing was starting to take a toll on Lucy's ears. Finally she pulled on a red dress with a band of black and silver sequins around her chest. Colleen cheered and clapped.

"Oh, yeah! That's it. That's the one." She stood behind Lucy and zipped her up. "My work here is done."

*   *   *

The dance started at eight; Lucy and Colleen arrived almost an hour and a half later. Colleen explained that they didn't want to look desperate, and by that time, the men would be bored with the women who'd been there all night. The grade school gymnasium was converted into a dance hall, with the basketball hoops tilted back and most of the bleachers recessed against the wall. Round brown tables circled the center of the court to form the dance floor. A snack table held soda and bowls of chips and pretzels. The few men stood across the room with their hands shoved into their pockets, mumbling conversations, staring at their shoes. Lucy stood in her dress and matching red sandals, her hair teased to almost the height of Colleen's. She felt the hair on her arms stand up, but saw only goose bumps. Her bare legs were in the same condition. Colleen had assured her that no one was wearing stockings these days.

Lucy thought she recognized some of the faces from her new neighborhood. She was grateful that she wasn't standing in her own grade school gymnasium, grateful that the men weren't huddled, chortling about "George of the Jungle." People in her old neighborhood had long memories.

"Not much has changed since high school, huh? Boys on one side, girls on the other," said Colleen.

"Yeah. I guess." It was fine with Lucy. As Colleen had predicted, this was just her speed.

"I bet that's even the same deejay." Colleen's eyes evaluated the crop of men in assembly.

Clusters of women braved the dance floor, wiggling their hips, scarcely lifting their feet off the floor as they glanced past each other to see if anyone of interest had arrived. Slow dances cleared the floor. When "It's Raining Men" played, women charged the floor, howling and jumping up and down. It struck Lucy as strange that they would do this in front of prospective dates. Colleen managed to drag Lucy into the center of the gym to dance, but Lucy didn't last very long. She didn't know how to dance and, while that didn't seem to inhibit the majority of people on the dance floor, it bothered her.

Most of the time, the two sat on an extended bleacher and Colleen gave Lucy the scoop on those in attendance. This was her neighborhood; she'd known everyone since before grade school. This one used to beat up the little runts, this one picked his nose, and this one was on the *Al Albert's Showcase*. She knew who had dated whom, who'd flunked out and had to go to public school, and where they all worked or no longer worked. Lucy was distracted by her toenails, which were painted the same red as her fingernails. She kept swinging her foot and watching reflections from the disco ball in their gloss.

"I'm going for a smoke." Lucy reached into her purse for her cigarettes and lighter.

"We just got here," Colleen said. "You haven't even talked to anybody yet."

"I've been talking to you and it's been an hour." Lucy said without turning back to look at her escort. She was fairly certain of the grimace on Colleen's face.

Lucy retreated out the nearest side exit and lit a cigarette. She leaned against the cool, stone wall of the school, her head back, eyes closed, and exhaled a long stream of smoke.

"Evening."

Startled, she jumped and knocked her head on a stone that jutted out just above her. Sitting on a low wall across from her was a man smoking a cigarette. A few years older than she was, he had his thick black hair cut short and parted on the side. His round face was clean-shaven, but she could still see the shadow of his beard.

"Hey." She rubbed the top of her head, then checked her fingers to see if there was any blood. None. She took another drag of her cigarette, then rubbed her bare, smooth forearm.

"Sorry about that. You okay?" He remained on the wall, wearing a concerned expression and then, finally, he let out a chuckle.

"My name's Tony Donato." He switched his cigarette to his left hand and extended his right.

Lucy shook his meaty hand. It made her own hand seem the size of a toddler's. "Lucy Pescitelli," she said with her eyes cast down.

"Nice to meet you." He flicked his cigarette and it traveled to the middle of the street in an arc. "I hate these things, don't you?" he said, tilting his head toward the gym.

"Oh, yeah," she said.

"My aunt helped organize it. She's real involved with the church, ya know?" he said. "She's always inviting me to things, since my folks practically live down the shore these days. Anyway, she begged me to come and bring along some of the guys. So here I am."

"That's nice," Lucy said. He was looking at her, really looking at her. Had she managed to ignite the hairspray Colleen had applied to her hair? She didn't smell anything. Nervously she rubbed her forearm, searching for the familiar.

"I haven't seen you before," he said.

"I'm new to the parish."

"So how'd you wind up here on a Saturday night?" He pulled another cigarette out of the pack with his lips. With one hand, he wrapped a match around to the back of the book and lit it with his thumbnail. His motions were so fluid.

"A friend brought me," she managed to get out. "I'd better go back in. She's by herself." She tossed her cigarette the way he had, but missed the mark.

He stood and opened the door for her. "Nice meeting you, Lucy Pescitelli."

She bent her head and passed under his arm and through the doorway, noticing his solid stocky body.

Inside, Colleen stood by the refreshment table. Lucy went straight for the ice bucket, avoiding looking at her. The ice rattled in the plastic cup; her hands were shaking. Get a hold of yourself, she thought. It was just a conversation. He's just a guy. But she knew it was a different kind of conversation. He had flirted with her.

Colleen edged closer to Lucy, "Excuse me, but I see panty lines. Did you change your panties?"

"I felt like a puppet on a string. Besides, I didn't want to be pulling at them all night."

"I suppose there is an adjustment period," Colleen said, glancing at Lucy then surveying the room. "What's up? Did you see a ghost out there?"

"No. Just a guy."

"That guy over there?"

Lucy turned around to see Tony walking toward them, a smile stretched across his face.

"Tony Donato?" Colleen asked, facing the table now.

"Colleen, I don't know what I'm doing," Lucy whispered.

"Dance with him. It's a start."

Tony stretched out his hand, "Do you want to dance?"

Colleen nudged her forward. It was the last dance of the evening, and couples suddenly appeared on the floor. Heatwave's "Always and Forever" blared through the loud speakers as he held her close enough that she could feel his body and smell his cologne. She rested her head on his shoulder and closed her eyes halfway. Somehow it made the tacky disco ball reflections bouncing off the cinder-block gymnasium walls romantic.

When the song ended, the lights came on, and Tony asked if he could escort Lucy home. "Well, I came with my friend," she answered.

As if on cue, Colleen walked toward them. "I'm beat, but why don't you stay out." Turning to Tony, she said, "Could you make sure she gets home safe?"

"Of course," said Tony.

Before Lucy could respond, Colleen pulled Lucy aside, "You'll be fine. Have fun."

As Tony folded tables, pushed the bleachers back against the wall, and said goodnight to his friends, Lucy helped his aunt clear the snack table. Anyone who would sacrifice a Saturday night to help his aunt assemble a Catholic singles dance, Lucy thought, couldn't be bad.

On the walk home, Lucy wished she had some antacid to calm her nervous stomach. Being with people, making conversation, smiling, exhausted her. Blisters were developing on her toes. When she teetered stepping off a curb, Tony took her hand and placed it on his arm. She liked the feel of his arm, the warmth of his body, the way he filled the silence with talk about the mildness of the evening, the impending heat of the upcoming summer. He asked where she went to school, where she worked. With each painful step bringing them closer to her doorstep, Lucy grew tenser with excitement, or dread, she couldn't tell which. No one had ever walked her home before. When they arrived at the house, it was late. The Delvecchio sisters were in for the night, their houses dark.

Just to be sure, she said in a whisper, "This is me."

"Already?" he said.

"Sorry."

He let go of her arm and rubbed the back of his neck. "Would you be up for making some coffee? Talking a bit more?"

"Here?" Lucy stood at the top of the stoop and opened the screen door.

"Never mind. Maybe another time." He stepped up on the bottom step.

As Lucy unlocked the door, she could feel his breath on her neck. He stood next to her and kissed the top of her head. "Does it hurt?"

She'd forgotten she'd banged it on the wall. "A little."

When she turned away from the door, he stretched his arms above her on the doorframe. He leaned down and kissed her on the mouth. She braced herself against the door and let him kiss her. His tongue moved back and forth across hers. She didn't respond, couldn't respond. He pulled back.

"I've been wanting to do that all night."

"I've gotta go," she said.

"You sure?"

"Yeah. Thanks." Lucy pushed the door open, quickly closed it behind her, then ran to the bathroom with her hand over her mouth. She managed to make it to the peach-colored toilet. In eighth grade, a boy named Lou, one of the popular boys, lost a bet with his friends. So, he had to kiss Lucy Pescitelli in the parking lot that was the schoolyard. He had run up to her, accosted her on the mouth with his lips, nearly knocking her over, and had run away. Laughter from the circle of boys amplified when, after she caught her balance, she wiped her mouth with her sleeve.

After several washings, there was no trace of mascara under her eyes. She could still smell his cologne. Had Tony lost a bet? She brushed her teeth for the second time and thought about the kiss, how completely unprepared she'd been. Just like with Lou. How frightened. Colleen knew she was a virgin, but probably hadn't guessed how much of a virgin. She took water into her mouth with her hand and swished it around, watching her cheeks alternately puff out. Colleen had forgotten to take after-pictures.

Chapter Ten

The following Thursday night, Lucy was surprised to see Tony waiting under the awning outside of Botti's Funeral Home. He stood with his hands in his pockets, his head down as he knocked his white sneakers together. They were luminous under the glow of the streetlight. She was impressed; he must have taken note of her hours during their brief walk home from the dance. He looked different now. As he opened the door for her, she noticed that his belly was a little larger, and he was shorter than she remembered. She knew she had to look different to him too, in her pants and flats and without Colleen's makeup and hair intervention. She locked up the funeral home and they went for coffee at the pastry shop around the corner. Lucy knew the owner. She knew most everyone in her old neighborhood. She'd witnessed all of them bury someone. As she and Tony walked, she said hello to several people. Tony must have thought her very social and popular. People did seem to like her; they just didn't ask her to dinner. She couldn't help but wonder if she gave off a strange vibe or whether it was just her job that put people off, as if she carried a death germ. Even if invited, she didn't know whether she'd have accepted. What would they have talked about?

Over cappuccinos and biscotti, which Tony ordered, they discussed the dance in more detail and with more honesty. Tony said how awkward and pathetic it was, how odd it was that they were both there. He told her he worked in the physical plant department at Temple University. She asked if he was afraid to work in North Philadelphia.

"Nah, I'm tougher than I look. You sort of got to be security, too, ya know."

Lucy did look at him and he didn't seem that tough. He seemed older than he had at the dance. Maybe it was the disco ball or the fumes of the Stardust goop, but he had seemed too handsome then, high-school-cool-crowd-handsome then. He was less intimidating now, and Lucy took comfort in that. She liked the relaxed softness to his face, as though it had finally settled in.

Tony talked in fits and spurts. Lucy spoke when asked questions. Yes, she had a sibling, a sister, they weren't that close. No, both her parents were dead. She lived alone. No, she didn't really like it.

His parents were alive and lately spent more of their time at their summer home in North Wildwood than in their house in South Philadelphia where Tony continued to live. He was the youngest of four, all boys. The rest were married with kids. At thirty-eight, he had never been married. He didn't like living alone, either.

Tony drove her home. "I really enjoyed talking to you, Lucy Pescitelli. I haven't met anyone like you in a long time. Ever, maybe."

"You need to spend more time in funeral homes." She was surprised when he laughed.

"Funny too." He gave her a kiss on the cheek before she got out of the car.

When Lucy got inside, she ran to the kitchen to call Colleen. She'd been on a real date, a short one, but a real one. And she had someone to talk about it with. She felt like she was playing catch-up with every normal thirteen-year-old girl or, she thought, does it even start earlier than that? She had a girlfriend and maybe a boyfriend as well.

"He's stalking you. You think that's romantic?" Colleen's response surprised Lucy. She thought that her friend's goal had been to get her a date, but Colleen seemed disappointed that Lucy was interested in Tony. It was as though she should have some say in whom Lucy dated, since she had packaged her for the world of singles. Or did her friend just see her as an oversized doll to dress up, primp, and prop up next to her. "You can do better," Colleen said.

"But you were the one who told me to dance with him. You were the one who told him to walk me home."

"That was one night. I didn't expect you to run off and elope with the first guy who noticed you."

"We didn't elope."

"I want you to have a little fun." Colleen paused. "I want to have a little fun with you."

As soon as Lucy hung up the phone, it rang. It was Tony asking if she was free Saturday night. She wondered if she'd passed some sort of a test over cappuccino. Had he compiled a list of questions to discern whether he wanted a woman? Lucy set Colleen's disapproval aside and planned to meet Tony again, but she felt like she was betraying her girlfriend. There were so few people in her life; it seemed strange that she always had to choose between them. First, between her mother and Anne, and now between Colleen and Tony, two people she barely knew.

* * *

The Italian restaurant was crowded on Saturday night. Lucy remembered the last time she'd been to a restaurant was for a bridal shower for her co-worker Ralph's wife, who was now pregnant with their third child. Tony and Lucy sat at a table near the bar. The noise of mingling conversations and moving dishes added to Lucy's exhilaration. She felt as if she'd been stand-ing on a train platform for years, watching other people come and go, and then suddenly she'd leapt onto it. She wasn't riding in a passenger car but bracing herself between cars, frantically trying to keep her balance, all the while enjoying the swaying, jerky movement of the train and the air rush-ing over her in gushes. She made an effort to look like she belonged at that candle-lit table, sitting across from a man, eating calamari, sipping Chianti. Even at that moment, she longed to tell Colleen every detail, but she hadn't even told Colleen about the date. Lucy didn't want to be pushed off the train.

"So your mother was Irish; did she cook Italian?" Tony asked. The wait-ress came and took the appetizer plate, which Tony had wiped clean with his bread.

"She mostly cooked Italian. My dad actually taught her, and she taught me. I can do the basics — you know, spaghetti and meatballs, lasagna, chicken cacciatore."

"Your dad could cook?" He handed her a cigarette. She leaned in and lit it with the candle he held for her.

"He was a bachelor for a long time. His mom died when he was born, so he had to learn," she said.

"I can't cook worth a damn. It's a real talent."

"It's not that hard, really."

"Don't sell yourself short there." He smiled.

Lucy realized then that Tony thought she was interesting, even accom-plished. She wished she could crawl into his head, look through his eyes, and see what he saw — a woman. An attractive woman. She thought of Colleen's comment, but inside Tony's head didn't seem scary or crazy. He was interested in her, in what she had to say, in whether or not she liked her dinner. He was interested.

He talked about her again. "You know, you're a rarity. Nobody takes care of family anymore. Your staying with your mother 'til the end, it just isn't done these days. I think it's really great." He took her hand just as the waitress appeared with their entrees. Their brief contact had startled Lucy. "My aunt was real impressed with you, too."

The food was delicious, but Lucy felt full already and didn't eat much. Tony ate systematically and with great concentration. He gathered his spaghetti around his fork, then attached it to a bite-size piece of chicken Parmesan he'd cut. Each mouthful was followed by a sip of wine. When he spoke again, it was about her job.

"Do you like it?" he asked, as he prepared another mouthful.

"It's not a bad job. Just some dusting and vacuuming, answering the phones. That kind of thing," she said. Tony slowly spun his fork, collecting pasta. "I don't deal with the dead people," she assured him.

"So you don't touch them? Or see them naked?"

"No, never."

Relieved, he leaned back in his chair and stretched his legs out under the table, one leg on either side of her crossed bare legs.

"Still, don't you get sad? It's kind of morbid, isn't it?"

"No, not really. Everyone dies, and people need to say goodbye." This was the first time Lucy had answered this question. She was surprised she had an answer, and surprised by what that answer was. "People need a place, some place neutral that doesn't hold all their memories. They need to see it's just a body." She rubbed her forearms. "It's just a body."

"That's kinda beautiful. What you said." Tony lifted his wine glass.

Lucy took a sip of wine and held it in her mouth, closed her eyes and slowly released the fluid down her throat. The perfume of the red wine permeated her nostrils. She felt the smoothness of her legs gliding past each other as she uncrossed them. Tony was looking at her, she knew. The restaurant gently swayed. This might be the most beautiful moment in her life. They agreed to have coffee back at her house.

*   *   *

It began on the couch where Tony kissed her for a long time. After a moment, Lucy responded without realizing it, as though she'd been kissing boys since adolescence. She was quite warm. His hands on her back, holding her to him, were even warmer; she could feel them through her cotton shirt. When he tried to recline her onto the sofa, the plastic covering was unforgiving and seemed to repel them back into an upright sitting position. They both felt it, the need to move. Tony took her by the hand and led her up the stairs. She followed him, knowing they were going to have sex. They were going to sin. Still, she didn't stop it, just as she hadn't stopped her mother's murder. Somewhere in the back of her mind, she rationalized this moment.

Tony was in charge. It was his idea; therefore, it was his sin. At the top of the stairs, he turned toward the front bedroom, and she pulled him back toward her room, and then stopped. Her pulling was participation, was a decision, and she didn't want to be responsible. Yet, she wanted it to happen, just not in her mother's bed.

"I thought you lived alone," he said.

"I do. The back room is quieter."

He didn't protest; he had other things on his mind. He led her into the back room and turned on the overhead light. She shook her head and pointed to the bedside lamp. He understood.

They were on the bed. Her body complied with his movements. He was on top of her, kissing her. That she could hardly breathe added to the intensity. It was going to happen. Sex. He undressed her and she scurried under the covers. He undressed himself and she closed her eyes, mostly, until he joined her under the covers. She put her arms around him; his upper back was smooth. Was that a sin, putting her arms around him? He kissed her neck, and then her breasts, one, then the other. She could feel her body moving, reacting. For a moment, she felt as if she had to go to the bathroom. Then she remembered the stories Marge had told her about girls having sex for the first time. There was the standard getting-pregnant-the-first-time tale, but Marge preferred the more subtle ones about girls losing control of their bladders and peeing all over the men. Or worse, the stories of girls nearly hemorrhaging to death, having to be rushed to the emergency room, and everyone finding out.

With his hand between her legs and his mouth still roaming her chest, Tony gained Lucy's full attention. He said nothing; there was no eye contact, but Lucy saw the serious concentration on his face. She didn't want to interrupt him with actions or words. He knew exactly what she needed.

Maybe he was taking advantage of her. She hadn't verbalized agreement; she hadn't verbalized disagreement. Neither yes nor no. Maybe when all was done, she could justify that she'd been seduced and vow never to have sex again. This could be her first step toward sainthood. It was nothing to give up sex if you'd never had it. Now, it would be a sacrifice. Besides, hadn't Marge always said the best saints were sinners first?

He was inside her. She held her breath. He tested her slowly. She felt herself stretching, but it wasn't as painful as she had expected. He was in completely. They didn't look at each other as she wrapped her arms around his neck and held on. He began to move like waves across her. She felt like a woman. When he finished, he relaxed the weight of his body down on top of hers. Her face was wet with silent tears that rolled onto her neck, cooling her. She reached up and buried her fingers in his thick black hair.

It was quiet. Lucy heard only his breathing. She began to copy the rhythm so that their bodies still moved together. Tony kissed her forehead.

"Can I stay?"

"Yes."

Once Lucy was confident that Tony had fallen asleep, she reached down and checked the sheets. They were relatively dry. She'd maintained control of her bladder and had managed not to hemorrhage. She hadn't done anything embarrassing. Her first sexual experience was complete and satisfying. Now she wondered if it would, or should, be her last.

This was the first night she'd slept next to anyone. Her head rested on his chest. Sleepiness came over her finally, and quieted her thoughts. Her senses took over. She enjoyed the physical presence of the man lying next to her — the salty smell of his perspiration mixed with his cologne, the stickiness between her legs, the sound of his breathing, her breathing. Under his chin was a line where his facial hair stopped. She ran her fingers along it, wondering if it stopped like that on all men. She caressed his chest and collarbones as if it were a nightly ritual that allowed her to fall asleep. She hadn't even realized that she was gently tugging at his forearm hair, until he murmured in his sleep and rolled over. This might only happen once. She was realistic, but she decided that she was undoubtedly in love, even if for just this moment, just this night. Someone had wanted her. She had loved.

Chapter Eleven

Tony had left by the time Jack arrived the next morning. As planned, he'd come over directly after Mass at St. Catherine's. There was water damage on the ceiling in the front bedroom, and he'd offered to fix it. Handyman jobs seemed to appeal to him more than the law. He had a reputation of showing up to write a will and fixing the kitchen sink instead. When he went upstairs to change out of his dress pants and oxford shirt and into jeans and a T-shirt, Lucy briefly envisioned him bare-chested. Then she replaced the image with Tony's chest, a chest she'd actually seen, felt, and slept on.

Sitting at the kitchen table while the coffee brewed, Lucy felt self-conscious. Even though she had showered and dressed, she thought he might know that she'd slept with someone the night before. The Sunday *Inquirer* was strewn across the table. Lucy read the magazine, Jack the real estate section. She was having trouble concentrating on the glossy pages and on Jack's occasional comments about the market in their neighborhood. Her thoughts kept returning to Tony, his smell, his touch. After pulling out the entertainment section, Jack looked at Lucy as if he were studying a room that had been rearranged, trying to figure out where the furniture used to be.

"You look different," he said, pouring their coffee.

"Oh?" Lucy focused on getting the string off the box of cinnamon buns Jack had brought. "I've missed these."

"The bakery's not that far." He helped pull the string to one side of the box. "Seriously, what's different?"

Lucy wasn't sure what to say. Had he noticed the changes Colleen had made to her? Or had he noticed the change Tony had made?

"I got a haircut," she fibbed.

"No. It's not that," he said. The box was open, and he got up to get a knife to cut the cinnamon buns. He turned and looked at her again. "You seem relaxed. Happy."

Lucy smiled unknowingly. He handed her a bun. "Thanks," she said.

Much to her relief, Jack changed the subject. He told her his Aunt Libby, Mrs. Garrity, said to say hello. Lucy hadn't heard from or seen her since the move. She'd thought the old woman had completely forgotten about her. Of course, Lucy hadn't contacted Mrs. Garrity either.

Lucy and Jack were quiet, the way people who have known each other a long time can be, biting into the sticky buns and wiping their chins. Jack's fingers, she noticed, were longer than Tony's, his hands narrower. He popped a stray raisin in his mouth. He was an attractive man; she hadn't realized or maybe she'd forgotten. Years ago, she had put him in the role of brother. Was it because he seemed so much older then? Or had he put her in the role of a sister first? His fair skin was ruddy and his wavy hair was slightly receded. He was textured in a comfortable way like a favorite worn sweater that you keep reaching for on winter mornings. She wanted to touch him, try him on.

Colleen had teased her about Jack the night of the dance. Did Jack want to have sex with her? What would that be like? Last night's sex was making her think this way. It had put a filter on the morning. Everything was sexual.

"So how do you like St. Catherine's? Father Burns can be a little long with the homilies, huh?" Jack had finished his bun. He leaned forward in his chair, crossed his long legs, and held his cup with both hands. His jeans were torn in spots and covered with paint and plaster residue.

"It's fine." Lucy hadn't been to church, any church, since Marge's Funeral Mass in November. Were his eyes always green? "I haven't been yet, really."

"Oh."

"Why do you go to church, Jack?"

"I don't know. Tradition," he said. "It gives me an hour to think each week."

That was just what Lucy feared — thinking about her mother in the presence of God. "Do you think my mother's in heaven?"

"Why not? She did her best." Lines formed in his forehead as he arched his right eyebrow. His green eyes peered over the rim of his cup as he sipped. "Is this related to your not going to church?"

"I don't know. Why don't we go look at that ceiling?"

Jack started toward the living room stairs and Lucy followed. At the bottom of the steps, he turned abruptly. Lucy had to stop short to avoid walking into him. "It's not the Church's fault that Marge left them the house," he said. "Don't stop going because of that."

"I know. You're right. I'll go again. I'm sure." The desire to rest her head against his chest and listen to his heartbeat came over her. She regretted asking him about her mother; she had only done it to distract herself, and it hadn't worked. Tomorrow, she thought, she'd be past thinking about sex. Tomorrow, Jack would be Jack again.

The damage to the ceiling ran across the front of the room above the windows and into the closet. Nothing had changed since Lucy had moved into the house. The front bedroom was, for the most part, as it had been in the old house, her mother's room. Jack remained silent on the subject until he opened the closet door.

"We're going to need to clear this out." He handed Lucy a hatbox from the shelf. "I can help you go through these things. Get them ready for St. Vincent's, if you want."

"I don't know," she said.

"Is Anne going to help with this?" He put another box on top of the first.

"No, she doesn't want anything." Lucy remained still.

"Has she called you?" he said.

"No. Why?"

"I just thought she might, you know, check in with you," he said. Something was up. Lucy could tell by his expression of forced nonchalance. The last box he placed came to Lucy's chin, so she carried them into the middle bedroom.

It only took two trips to the middle bedroom to carry Marge's clothes from the closet. Jack started moving the furniture out of the way. They removed the drawers from Marge's dresser and brought them to the other room, so they could slide the dresser away from the closet. Lucy left Jack alone to work, once the room was ready and she'd refreshed their coffees.

Marge's things, her life, it seemed, lay before Lucy. She sat on the bed and lit a cigarette. When she'd come to look at the house, it was empty, so she didn't know what function this room had had. The middle room was Anne's room. Lucy had assembled it as it had been in the old house, with the exception of the David Bowie and Prince posters Anne had left thumbtacked to the walls. They were rolled up in the closet. The previous homeowners had wallpapered the room. The pattern was broad purple and orange stripes with thin reflective silver stripes separating them. If she spun around quickly, she was certain she'd have the sensation of being on a Tilt-A-Whirl at a traveling carnival. Anne's pale yellow, floral bedspread clashed with the wallpaper. It didn't make sense to keep it — the bedspread or the wallpaper.

Gazing over Marge's clothing, Lucy realized that her mother's favorite color must have been kelly green. Jack was hammering the plaster. She could hear it falling. The house was coming down. She felt Marge in the room. Marge knew. As Lucy finished her cigarette and began taking the house dresses off the hangers and folding them, she decided they couldn't stay in the house after she'd brought a man into her bed. Not once in the past that Lucy could recall had she misbehaved in her mother's house, among her mother's things. Marge never stated that sex was bad or immoral. Instead, she focused on the tragic results — pregnancy, disease, parenthood. But Lucy knew her mother would not approve. Today, her mother's things needed to be gone. Jack was here. He could take them to St. Vincent's so that she wouldn't have to.

There were other dresses that Lucy couldn't recall her mother wearing. As children, Lucy and Anne had never played dress-up with their mother's things; they weren't allowed in their parents' bedroom. These dresses were for special occasions, most were floor length, clingy but modest, from the seventies. Lucy wondered why Marge had bothered to keep them. But Marge had kept everything of hers. It occurred to Lucy that her mother had nothing from her own childhood. How quickly had Marge had to leave her parents' home? Did she decide to take only the necessities? It seemed that in the late sixties, her mother had sprung into her new life like a weed through cracks in cement, no roots. Still, why keep these seemingly meaningless items? Perhaps, her mother had thought of this moment, of her daughter sifting through outfits trying to assign them meaning when there was none. Lucy pulled a black dress off its wire hanger. The shoulders were misshapen. As she laid it flat on the bed and tried to press the bumps down, she realized that it was the dress Marge had worn to Joseph's funeral.

Lucy had been devastated when her father died. There were only a few people she'd loved, and none of them had ever died before. Her father's death was unexpected. She remembered her mother taking her by the hand to say her final farewell. Lucy stood over her father's casket; the kneeler had been removed already. Marge pulled Joseph's hammer from her oversized purse and placed it in the casket by his hip where he always wore it. His death had strengthened Lucy's faith in the afterlife, in God. His body, so still, so stiff, was an obvious shell. It was his soul that she loved and that was gone. There was no doubt in her mind that Joseph went directly to heaven. To Lucy, he had been only goodness: but she was just seventeen when he died. Time might have revealed more about him to her. Maybe she would have worried about his final destination just as she worried about Marge's.

Lucy folded the dresses neatly on the bed, and began emptying the drawers. Her mother's shirts and cotton pants were worn, but clean and never in disrepair. She wondered if anyone would want them. They wouldn't fit her. Marge had been tall and thin; Lucy was short and full-bodied. For a fleeting moment, she thought of Anne. She couldn't imagine Anne wearing anything of Marge's. The clothes could only be her mother's.

How had Anne handled their deaths? Anne had abandoned religion in college. Instead of strengthening her faith, had Joseph's death had the opposite effect on her sister? That happened, Lucy knew from attending so many wakes. Death brought out the extreme in people. Either their loved ones were taken into the arms of a benevolent God who loved them, or their loved ones were yanked from life by a cruel and unjust God. Either way, God was usually involved. What explanation did Anne have?

Lucy turned away from the piles on the bed and left to check on Jack. He'd begun applying new plaster to the ceiling. He stood tall on the ladder. Though he had a tendency to curl up while sitting, he had impeccable posture when standing. He agreed to drop Marge's things off at the charity. Lucy bagged them and placed them by the front door. She wondered if anything of her father's was left, or if Marge had given it all away. It was strange that Marge would leave everything of hers to be gone through, to be weighed in value, and nothing of Joseph's. She shed whole phases of her life in order to take on new roles — wife, mother, widow.

At lunch, Jack came into the kitchen after washing up. White powder clung to the edges of his face and in spots on his arms. As they sat to eat reheated soup, the phone rang. It was Tony, and Lucy felt embarrassed taking the call in front of her old friend. Jack delicately sipped his soup and rummaged through the untouched newspaper sections in an effort to give her privacy. Tony wanted to see her that night. She turned her back from Jack, faced the bags of Marge's clothes in the living room, and said yes.

Chapter Twelve

When Lucy came out of the basement carrying the laundry basket, she saw Colleen's fair, freckled legs hanging over the arm of Marge's chair. She was positive she'd never seen her mother reclined in the same fashion. The posture was altogether too carefree. The sight of Colleen was not surprising; after all, she regularly let herself in on weekdays that she didn't work. On those mornings, she always found Lucy in the kitchen, getting breakfast. But generally on weekends, Colleen slept late and then spent the rest of the day entertaining Tiffany.

The front window was open a few inches, because last night the weatherman had promised a warm day — finally, but the temperature dawdled in the low fifties. From Colleen's short denim skirt and chunky-heeled flip-flops, Lucy assumed she had seen the same forecast. Goosebumps covered her forearms and legs.

"I thought you were in the bathroom." Colleen wiggled further into the chair. "I'm surprised how comfortable this is. You'd never know it by looking at it."

"Laundry," Lucy said, holding the laundry basket out as proof before placing it on the couch. Tony was in the bathroom. Despite Colleen's frequent visits, Lucy hadn't mentioned her dates with Tony. Colleen did most of the talking anyway, and Lucy anticipated that Colleen wouldn't be excited for her, especially since she'd called Tony a stalker. In the speckled mirror, she watched her friend's legs sway back and forth, her flip-flops dangling off her toes. Lucy looked in the laundry basket for something of hers to fold. Part of her wanted to keep their relationship a secret, free from the scrutiny that she was certain Colleen would add. Tony was completely positive, never complaining, so pleased with anything and everything Lucy did. It was refreshing.

"Well, obviously. I can see that now," Colleen said as she pulled herself up on her elbows. "Anyway, the asshole's got Tiffany for the weekend. Did I tell you that? He's got some cousin in upstate New York getting married, so they won't be back until tomorrow night."

"That's nice. You've got some time to yourself." The load of laundry was whites, and mostly Tony's undershirts and boxers. One of his first admissions of weakness to Lucy was that he was terrible at doing laundry. He'd asked if she could show him how to do it properly. His mother had tried, he said, but it never stuck. Lucy volunteered to do it for him and the precedent was set. Besides, she liked doing something for him, and he was very appreciative. Still, Lucy kept her back to Colleen as she folded his items; she piled them on the other side of the basket, out of her friend's view.

After a few moments of silence, Colleen pulled herself out of the chair. "So. What do you want to do?" She stood seemingly ready to leave with Lucy at that very moment.

"What? Now?" Lucy quickly put another pair of boxers on top of the pile.

"Yeah. Why not? Two free, single women out on the town."

"I wish you'd given me some warning, is all." Lucy was nearing the bottom of the basket, just her underwear and Tony's sweat socks left to fold.

"Well, I can wait for you to shower and dress. Maybe we should go shopping, get you something to wear that's not black. I'm surprised to see so much white." Colleen tugged a sweat sock from Lucy's hand.

"I'm kinda busy." Lucy didn't know why she said that. She needed to tell Colleen the truth. Besides, Tony and she didn't have any specific plans; maybe she could spend some time shopping.

"You can do wash another day. Come on. It's beautiful out. Don't spend the day inside cleaning. Let's have fun." Colleen pulled two sweat socks from Lucy's hands as she was pairing them up. From outside, they could hear the Delvecchio sisters exiting their houses, screen doors banging closed, and making their way down their steps with their lawn chairs. "Even the Delvecchios are going out." Colleen looked down and saw what she was holding. "Lucy, are you taking in laundry? Do you need money?"

Lucy laughed. "No, and no."

"So you're wearing boxers now?"

"Yes," she said. "They're much more comfortable than those thongs. You should try them."

"Ha." Colleen smirked, crossed her arms in front of her, and waited for an explanation.

"They're Tony's," Lucy said. Colleen looked confused, as if she hadn't understood the words Lucy spoke. "Tony Donato's," Lucy said as she turned and put the piles of laundry into the basket. The cranky murmurs of the Delvecchio sisters came through the window on a cool breeze. They knew about Tony. As Lucy came and went from the house, they made comments about what time Tony left, if he left. Surely, Colleen had to have heard the gossip. She couldn't be so surprised.

"I don't understand. Why are you doing his laundry?" Colleen finally spoke.

"We're dating."

"You're dating? What? For two seconds, and he's got you doing his laundry?"

This was what Lucy had suspected her friend's reaction would be. Negative. But why dress up for them, then? Why go to a dance or a club to meet them? "It's no big deal."

"Lucy, can't you let yourself have any fun?"

They heard the bathroom door open.

"He's here?" Colleen whispered.

"Yes." Lucy looked up into the mirror as Tony came down the stairs, newspaper folded under his arm, and saw Colleen step away from her as though they'd been embracing.

Tony slowed as he came to the bottom of the staircase. "Oh, hi. Colleen, right?"

"Tony." Colleen said, rubbing the goosebumps on her arms.

Lucy picked up the laundry basket to take it upstairs, but Tony came to her side, put his arm around her waist, and kissed her cheek. The smell of his cologne was warm and familiar. Lucy put down the basket.

"Beautiful day, huh?" Tony said to Colleen.

She smirked and shook her head. "That's just what I was saying."

"Did you already have breakfast? We were just about to have some. We're getting a late start. Or, I guess, I'm getting a late start."

"Sure. Coffee would be great." Colleen started for the kitchen.

"I'll just run this upstairs," Lucy said.

In her bedroom, Lucy could hear the sound of their voices in the kitchen below, but couldn't understand what they were saying. Tony's empty duffle bag was next to her bureau. She spread it on the bed and carefully placed his piles of clothing inside. What were they talking about? She imagined them in high school, sitting in bunches on the front steps leading to the row of gray metal entry doors, both in one of the cool crowds, no doubt. Tony, she imagined, corrupted the school uniform of khakis, white oxford, and navy tie with a denim jacket and metal-toed black boots. There, on the steps smoking with his buddies, they'd talk about drag racing on 61st Street. Not far away, maybe on the other side of the wide cement steps, Colleen sat with her girlfriends, her hair teased out, wearing big square aquamarine earrings, black eyeliner, and lace fingerless gloves. She was animated as she told stories about sneaking into bars on South Street and flirting with guitar players. Meanwhile, Lucy weaved her way through the clusters of teenagers into the building, grateful to be unnoticed.

Only Lucy's small stack of underwear remained in the laundry basket. Folded, they resembled tiny envelopes, personalized stationery. She'd graduated from high school twelve years ago. Why then, each time she envisioned what these new people in her life were like before she met them, did she return to the arena of high school? Tony and Colleen weren't even in high school at the same time. As she slid her underwear drawer closed, she realized the reason. High school was the last time she was with people her own age, her last reference point to her peers.

In the kitchen, Colleen and Tony sat on opposite sides of the tiny table. The empty chair in between them waited for Lucy. Instead of sitting, she began pulling food from the fridge.

"What do you want? French toast, eggs?"

"Whatever you're having," Colleen said.

"Oh, you know what I want," Tony said.

A subtle snort came from Colleen. Whatever they had talked about hadn't gone well.

"I already ate," Lucy said, "so it's whatever you want."

"I don't want you cooking for me if you've already eaten," Colleen said, even though ordinarily this was not a problem for her. "So, do you two have plans today?"

"I thought I'd take Lucy for a drive."

"Really. Where?" Colleen said.

"FDR Park," Tony said to Colleen, then turned to Lucy. "How's that sound?"

"That sounds nice. Would you be up for that, Colleen?" Lucy asked. They were quiet and Lucy didn't turn around. It was being decided in silence behind her. She unwrapped the sausages and placed two in the frying pan.

"No. Thanks. I'm going to head out. I've got lots to do," Colleen said, pushing the chair back, dragging it against the floor. "Maybe I'll come by tomorrow," she said to Tony as if to warn him. "I'll let myself out." Her flip-flops slapped across the kitchen floor until she reached the carpet.

Once they heard the screen door close, Tony came to the counter where Lucy stood cutting an onion. He wrapped his arms around her waist and rested his chin on her shoulder.

"What was that about?" Lucy asked, wiping a tear away with the back of her hand.

"What do you mean?" Tony squeezed her.

"Do you two hate each other?"

"No. We barely knew each other," Tony said, releasing her waist. He reached past her and opened the kitchen window. Marge's recipe box teetered on the narrow sill, but Tony caught it before it fell. "Are you real close with her?"

"She's my best friend." Lucy was surprised to hear herself use that term.

"I don't know, Luce. You know she trapped that poor guy."

"That's a terrible thing to say." Lucy tossed the chopped onion in the pan and grabbed a green pepper. Why was it that no one called this man — the asshole, that poor guy — by name.

"Everyone in the neighborhood knows that. They say it might not even be his." Tony leaned against the fridge, calmly sipping his coffee.

"She." Lucy gutted the pepper over the trash can.

"Huh?"

"They have a daughter. Her name is Tiffany."

"Oh."

As Lucy chopped, she knew there was a good possibility that what Tony said was true. But she liked Colleen. Colleen had pursued Lucy, something that no one else had done before. Maybe Colleen was so eager to befriend her because she wasn't from the neighborhood. Lucy understood that need better than Colleen could know. The sausages began to sizzle in the frying pan. They smelt good, and Lucy wished she'd made enough for herself too. What would people say about her? How would Tony react? How would Colleen? She was just starting to be this new Lucy, one without a mother, one with a friend, and a boyfriend.

"Just be careful with that one. That's all I'm saying." Tony pushed himself off the refrigerator and sat at the table.

"Sure," Lucy said, not knowing exactly what that would entail. As she placed a roll on his plate, he kissed her. She liked that he frequently pecked her on the cheek and hugged her as she stood at the sink or stove. "I'll be careful."

Chapter Thirteen

In Lucy's old neighborhood, young women pushed umbrella strollers, their wrists laden with multiple plastic bags. Old women pulled upright shopping carts; their solitary paper bags shifted about inside. On stoops and in doorways, men peered under their hat rims and over their folded newspapers to watch the women weave through the crowded sidewalks. Lucy smiled silent greetings at familiar faces. Stores were the same as when she was a child, except for the few that were abandoned, but with their signage still intact as a reminder, not replaced. Working in her old neighborhood was not the same as living there. After her evening shifts, most places were closed. People were at home, having already finished their dinners and settled in front of their televisions for the night.

Lucy had covered Ralph's morning shift at the funeral home because he was accompanying his wife to an ultrasound appointment. Gertie Hall, mother and wife, was buried. At the viewing, her grandchildren displayed a collage they had made of pictures taken throughout her life. She was one of those women who became prettier with age, like Jessica Tandy. Next to her husband of over sixty years, she'd dreamt and died. Bud and all eight children survived her, but Lucy thought that Bud probably wouldn't live much longer. Couples like Gertie and Bud were attached by an almost tangible cord that held them together, linked them between lives, and insisted on their prompt reunion.

Lucy decided to walk home through the old neighborhood instead of taking the bus home. Gertie and Bud's marriage, or Lucy's idea of it, had inspired her. Perhaps longevity had nothing to do with romance, but Lucy thought it might. Tony was coming over after work for dinner, as he did every evening Lucy was off. He usually stayed over, except when his parents were in Philadelphia. Then they might see each other, but he always went home at the end of the night. He said he didn't want his folks to think badly of Lucy. Lucy agreed. She was guilty. Already she suffered the snide, slightly muffled comments the Delvecchios volleyed back and forth to each other when they caught her leaving the house. What would the Donatos think? Lucy wasn't naïve; she watched television and knew the rest of the world was sleeping around. Some parents didn't care if their children had premarital sex. Some parents were having extramarital sex. In South Philadelphia, however, parents had the option of imagining their children as pure. Their daughters were virgins because, out of respect, they never gave the appearance of anything to the contrary. And still, she hadn't gone to confession; she wasn't ready to confess murder and she wasn't ready to stop having sex with Tony.

In Rose's card store, the smell of dust, fake flowers, and wax fruit overwhelmed Lucy's nostrils. Romance as seen on TV required candles. Rose knelt in the aisle, marking prices on figurines of animals dressed in occupational garb. An owl dressed as a teacher, a pig as a butcher. Dust collectors is what Marge called them.

"Hey, Lucy. Where you been? It's been ages," said Rose. Her hair was piled high on her head in the style she'd worn since the height of her beauty, though its sheen had faded.

"I moved over to St. Catherine's," Lucy said as she helped pull Rose off the floor. Rose's husband had died some time ago, but he hadn't yanked her into the afterlife yet. Rose wasn't going anywhere.

"What can I do for you?"

"Do you have candles?"

"Scented? I've got 'em all. Spiced apple. Ginger. Lavender. Great for the bathroom." Rose pointed to a shelf of thick squat candles the size of soup cans.

"Do you have any regular candles? For the dinner table?" Lucy blushed. She envisioned the candles in wine bottles, dripping wax over the labels and the wicker basket bottoms, and creating the perfect non-scented lighting. She'd seen it somewhere and that was what she wanted.

"I'll check in the back."

While Rose looked for candles, Lucy slowly walked up and down the store's three aisles. Rose was having a clearance sale, so the shelves were almost empty. Boxes of new inventory were stacked in the aisles. Lucy mentally searched her house for candles as she unconsciously perused items on display, touching some. She hadn't bought candles and Marge didn't have any, Lucy was almost confident.

Her parents' relationship became stranger to Lucy the longer they were both dead. She believed theirs was a good relationship, that they'd loved each other. They worked well together, moving about each other with precision but not grace — a well-choreographed dance, but not a tango. At times, there seemed a desperate need for each other, not romantically or sexually, but on a base human level that Lucy couldn't quite figure out.

Rose emerged empty-handed. "Sorry, hon. I'm out. I should have some early next week."

"Don't worry about it," Lucy said.

"How's your sister?" she asked, looking around. "She's married, right? Any kids?"

"Not yet."

"I guess these days, you girls aren't in any hurry. How 'bout yourself? Anyone special?" Rose found the price marker and slowly lowered herself to the floor again.

"No, not really." Lucy walked to the door. "Thanks again."

Since her mother's death, Lucy's view of life had gotten longer. Marge had not been a dreamer, at least as long as Lucy had known her. One day's index card of chores followed another. Life was about specific, manageable tasks. At Lucy's age, Marge was the mother of two and had been married a dozen years. Her life was settled. Lucy imagined herself as a woman older than Marge had lived to be, a woman like Gertie, laid out in the mauve dress and matching waistcoat she'd worn to her wedding anniversary party. For the first time, it seemed plausible, imaginable, that Lucy might have that, might be a wife, a mother, a grandmother. Would it bring her happiness?

Awnings — dark green, maroon, some striped — fluttered over the store fronts as Lucy walked and tried to think of another place that sold candles. The flower shop that supplied the funeral home was ahead. Upon opening the door, Lucy breathed flowers, a real smell — life, slightly chilled filling the tiny corner shop. Of course, she was used to being around flowers, working at the funeral home, but here, it was only the fragrance of petals and water drops. The scent of final preparation was missing. While Frank, the shop owner, was busy helping another customer, Lucy stopped at each bundle and inhaled deeply; it was more satisfying than a cigarette. Her own breath, she felt, didn't belong there, wasn't good enough to occupy the same space as the flowers' exhalations. She caressed their petals gently, apologetically; they were cool, pink, moist, and soft. They reminded her of the feel of her face just after waxing.

She purchased a dozen red roses; they were what she imagined she needed to set the scene. When Frank asked what the occasion was, Lucy said she just felt like having flowers in the house, which was partially true. Her mother never did. "Why do you want to buy something that's already dying?" she'd say.

The liquor store was around the corner. Lucy bought a jug of red wine and then headed back to the funeral home. Tony would be at the house soon and Lucy wanted to have everything ready when he arrived. No one was at the funeral home when Lucy let herself in. She took a box of long white candles from the storage closet and promptly left. She wasn't worried about being caught with them; she was worried about explaining why she had them. Something about the day — Gertie's pictures, the fluttering awnings, the dew on the flowers — was filling her with an odd and unexpected sensation of lighthearted hope. She hailed a cab.

*   *   *

The tub was three-quarters size and squished in the corner behind the door as if an afterthought. Lucy sat on the toilet lid smoking, plotting her first attempt at romance, and trying not to remember vomiting after her first kiss. The flowers, wine, and candles were on the floor. Unlike the peach tile, which ran half way up the walls and matched the toilet and sink, the forest-green bathmat and shower curtain worked well with the red roses. She flushed the cigarette butt down the toilet, took off her blouse, got on her knees, and scrubbed the tub in her bra and black pants. Since she started having Tony over, she hadn't cleaned as much. There wasn't as much time and, oddly, now that someone was actually visiting, the appearance of the house mattered less.

In the linen closet, Lucy found a bottle of bubble bath she'd been given as a party favor at a bridal shower years ago. She turned on the hot water and poured in the bubble bath. While the water ran, Lucy went downstairs to retrieve empty bottles for candleholders. Upon seeing her reflection in the gold-flecked mirror, she wrapped her arms around her breasts. She thought she looked like a wayward teenage babysitter in a stalker movie. After collecting an armful of wine and vinegar bottles, she arranged them around the bathroom, then pressed the funeral candles into their necks. The roses she placed in the vase on top of the radiator cover, with the exception of two. She pulled the petals off those to sprinkle about the floor.

There was cleanser on her elbows and belly. Strands of hair had fallen out of a broad clip at the base of her neck. When she touched her face, her fingers smelt of roses. Her skin was flush from the activity and looked healthy. While she didn't wear makeup or tease her hair as Colleen had done the night of the dance, she had kept up with the Stardust system. The smooth feel of her skin made her aware of her own body and made it seem new, capable of doing and enjoying things the old one hadn't.

After she washed up and put her shirt back on, she lit the candles and turned off the bathroom light. The room was just as she had imagined and she was proud of her handiwork. It looked just like a movie set, except everything was on a smaller scale.

Tony arrived at the expected time, talking as he entered the front door. "You'll never believe what that guy Gus did at work today." He wrapped one arm around Lucy and kissed her on the mouth. "I gotta go to the bathroom." He moved up the stairs, Lucy behind him. "We're sitting outside on the wall eating our lunch and these kids sit across from us." As he arrived at the bathroom door, Lucy stopped on the steps.

"Ah, Luce, this is real nice."

"Thanks."

"I just gotta move these two for a minute." He placed two candles on the floor and lifted the toilet lid. Lucy sat on the step. She didn't like to be reminded of the dual purpose of the penis.

"What's the occasion?" He flushed the toilet and replaced the candles.

"No occasion. I just thought it would be nice." She joined him in the bathroom.

"It is." They embraced.

Her efforts produced the desired reaction — he kissed her, began to undress her — things progressing as she intended. But Lucy wasn't lost in the romance. When he slid her unbuttoned blouse off her shoulders and let it drop to the ground, she flinched, then checked that it hadn't ignited on one of the candles. Awkwardly, she repositioned their bodies away from the flames while they disrobed. He'd managed to completely undress himself and was almost done with her. He tugged at the waistband of her stockings, having let her pants drop around her ankles. She rolled them down, hopping slightly on alternate feet as she pulled them free. Her belly was carved with seam lines and she cursed herself for not changing into something, anything, else. That she hadn't planned well bothered her, even if Tony didn't seem to notice the imperfections. When he kissed her where her neck met her shoulder, his scruff gently scratching her, she let her head fall forward and her shoulders drop. The warm sensation of skin next to skin was still an unexpected pleasure to her.

Slowly, the two submerged into the tub holding each other with one hand, the tub with the other. When they reached bottom, water sloshed over the edge, splashing on the floor.

"I got it." Tony pulled the bath towels, Marge's towels, off the rack and tossed them down. "Drain some water out."

Lucy reached under her backside to pull the plug. She'd been aware of it and its chain since the moment she sat down, but there was no room to move. Her elbow hit the faucet as she yanked it; her bone rang. The drain sucked on her rear end and made a raunchy, gurgling sound. And sound carried well in the small tiled room. There was always music in the movies. Why hadn't Lucy thought of it? What would she have played? "Always and Forever"? They didn't have a song of their own. How long did it take for that to happen? Tony preoccupied himself with opening the wine. Lucy leaned to one side to quiet and quicken the pace of drainage. A radio in the bathroom was not a good idea, she concluded. It would fall in the tub. They would be electrocuted. Their pruny bodies would be discovered, bobbing in the stagnant water, amidst dead flowers and burnt-down candles. Lucy replaced the plug.

The red wine glugged as Tony poured it into the glasses Lucy held. A splash of wine landed on top of the floating bubbles, turning them a bruised purple color. With the faucet situated behind her, Lucy needed to lean her head forward so that her chin was submerged in suds. His knees were up against his chest, since his legs were too long to stretch out. Lucy resituated, pushing her knees down and accidentally, ever so slightly, kicked him in his manliness. They both released nervous laughs, then leaned forward, more water pouring over the side, and, without injury, kissed.

The grating ring of the rotary phone sounded from the front bedroom, her mother's room. The two smiled at each other and shrugged it off. Lucy tried placing her feet on the outside perimeter of the tub. The phone kept ringing. Tony's feet slid under her, his toenails scraping her bottom. Lucy winced. He must have had better tub sex than this in his past. The phone kept ringing. When Tony finally stood, it was apparent that his interest in sex had waned.

"Could be something important." He stepped out of the tub and shook his body like a dog, then left a trail of suds into the hallway. Lucy gulped the remainder of her wine and submerged her head under the water. Now, it seemed to her that there wasn't just something failing in her romantic scheming but with their relationship. Tony must have been in love before. Lucy never asked because she feared being compared to his first love, a high school love perhaps, more beautiful, more passionate than Lucy, even if it was only the passage of time that made her so. Of course, this first love was tall, thin, blonde — Lucy wasn't immensely creative — with straight white teeth and perky breasts, unlike Lucy's, which she knew would more and more grow to resemble eggplants as she aged. Had he given her number to someone? When she resurfaced, Tony was calling her.

"It's your sister."

"Coming."

Next to the wet towels, their clothes lay absorbing excess water. Lucy flicked the suds off her body and got out of the tub. The candles were dwindling, their discarded wax running down the sides of the bottles and pooling on the tiles. One hand covering her crotch, the other holding her breasts together, she entered the hallway and opened the linen closet. Tony laughed. At the foot of the bed, he sat rubbing his hands through his hair, spraying sudsy water on her mother's good bedspread. She tossed him a towel.

"Anne?" Lucy stood drying herself with one hand. Tony didn't bother, merely draping the towel over his midsection.

"Lucy, did Mom send you anything?" Anne's voice was quavering as though she was about to cry.

"What do you mean? When?" Lucy sat. Tony reached under her towel and fondled her breasts.

"Did you get anything in the mail?" Anne asked.

"No," Lucy said. Tony knelt behind her. His towel was on the floor. "Are you okay?" His penis was hard against her back.

"Did Mom say anything about Dad? Before she died?"

"No." Lucy swatted at Tony and mumbled for him to stop. "What do you mean?"

"Never mind." Anne hung up.

Lucy dropped her hand with the receiver to her lap. She should call Anne back. As she reached for her mother's purse on the bedpost to retrieve the address book, Tony was on top of her and then inside her, too quickly for her to protest the place or time. Her romantic evening was officially a nightmare. The phone began to beep, begging to be hung up, to be put out of this uncomfortable situation. Her sister on the phone. Sex on her mother's bed.

Afterwards, Tony lay next to her. Lucy hung up the phone. She'd call Anne later. Maybe. What could Marge have sent Anne? Had Marge planned another betrayal? If Marge was capable of kicking her daughter out on the street, she could surely expose her as a murderer. Lucy couldn't predict her dead mother's actions.

Tony rolled over, sound asleep. That a man had answered the phone in Lucy's house had escaped her sister's notice or comment. But then, his presence wouldn't surprise Anne. She'd had boyfriends since high school, Brad since college. She was a feminist. Premarital sex was inconsequential to her.

As she drained the tub, Lucy sat on the toilet lid, smoking. She'd have to scrape the wax off the floor and counter later, but for now she held a single rose and inhaled its scent between drags on the cigarette, listening to the water drain out, and the man snoring in the room next door.

Chapter Fourteen

The bricks of the house held the unusual June heat. Sweat dotted Lucy's
T-shirt, even though the most physically stressful thing she'd done was
fill the coffee pot with water. Marge's index cards dictated that Thursday
was market day. Lucy took Marge's canvas shopping bag from the closet
(the one with butterflies that read: "If you love something set it free . . .").
Colleen arrived on the stoop as Lucy locked the front door. They exchanged
"heys" as if they'd just spoken yesterday. It had been a few weeks since they'd
talked over Tony's clean laundry.

Lucy understood that she had been given the silent treatment, that their
friendship was on Colleen's terms. It was Colleen who came to Lucy's house
when she wanted to talk. It was Colleen who decided what they should do.
And Colleen's absence was a sign of her disapproval of Lucy's dating or
Lucy's boyfriend. Lucy just couldn't be sure of which. For certain, Colleen
assumed that she was in charge, never considering the fact that Lucy hadn't
contacted her either. Despite what Tony had said about Colleen, Lucy missed
her friend. There were times in the past few weeks that she thought of dropping by Colleen's, but she hadn't, because Colleen would still be angry or
hurt, or whatever it was that had happened in the kitchen that day. Or Tony
would see them together and disapprove, thinking Colleen a bad influence.

Still, she was flattered that Colleen, standing there with her red nylon bag, remembered the Thursday shopping ritual. The Delvecchio sisters sat in their lawn chairs, their tall glasses of iced tea sweating next to them.

"Getting a late start," one said.

"When did he leave this time?" the other added. Lucy and Colleen ignored the elderly women.

Neither Lucy nor Colleen apologized. It was as if they had fought bitterly and with skill, knowing each other's weaknesses, but were the only kids of the same age on the block. If they wanted to go out and play, they had no choice but to make up. Besides, Lucy enjoyed the company. It was nice not to have to go shopping by herself; the mundane became social, an occasion to talk and laugh. Sometimes Colleen tried to haggle or even flirt to get discounts, and Lucy taught Colleen about getting the right cuts of meat, and which fruits and vegetables were in season. They had no choice but to forgive and forget.

For most of Lucy's life, friendship had been a spectator sport. When Lucy was a child, Marge would tell her to go outside and play when Mrs. Garrity came over for coffee and gossip. On the front stoop, Lucy would comb her doll's hair or color in a book. She was never athletic. Anne, on the other hand, would be in the center of the street, directing the other children on how to properly play stickball. The occasional stray ball would head toward Lucy, she would duck out of the way, most times, and the ball would bang against the aluminum screen door, then bounce back to the street. Marge would come running to the door, swing it open, almost knocking Lucy off the steps, and yell, "Cut it out! Take it somewhere else. Can't I get a moment's peace?" Of course, they couldn't take it somewhere else; they weren't allowed off the block.

Lucy's father frequently got himself in trouble when he'd hit a few balls with the kids after he came home from work. Joseph never hit a window or a door, but a few times he sent a ball on top of a roof. The kids would complain that they had no balls left. The next day he'd arrive home with a tube of brand new tennis balls for them. While the kids loved this, Marge didn't; he shouldn't have been encouraging her daughter to hang out with boys, hitting balls.

One time a ball landed on the Pescitellis' roof and settled on top of the bathroom skylight. Marge complained until Joseph borrowed a ladder from work and hiked up the side of the house to retrieve it. Everyone gathered out front to watch him climb up except Lucy. Alone, she stood in the bathroom looking up, waiting for her father. She saw his hands first, then his face as he leaned over the skylight. His stomach protruded slightly from his undershirt, revealing his cavernous navel. He smiled at her as he held up the ball, triumphant. Then he tossed the ball, crying "incoming" to the cheering crowd below. He looked down at Lucy again and in the muck on the exterior glass, he drew a heart and wrote Lucy's name in the center.

When she saw it, Marge threatened to send him up there all over again. But it stayed there, with Marge complaining, until a good rainfall washed it away. Lucy sat on the bathroom floor under the thundering sound of the storm on the glass pane and watched the raindrops erase her name.

Since Lucy fell in love, she wondered what drew her parents together in the first place. What had kept them together?

As they stood at a corner waiting for the light to change, Lucy noticed Colleen staring at her. The look was different from her typical "how could I improve upon this" one. Lucy turned and, having regressed to that awkward child relegated to the stoop, said, "Take a picture. It'll last longer." Lucy opened her eyes wide.

"You did the dirty," Colleen said.

"What?" Lucy said. There wasn't any filter between Colleen's mind and mouth. Momentarily, Lucy considered that she might appear physically altered, but then she realized that Colleen's comment was intended to embarrass her. Of course, Colleen knew they'd slept together. Tony was in Lucy's house early on a Saturday morning, and Lucy had already completed a load of laundry. Colleen was re-establishing who was boss.

"I hope you used protection. You don't know where he's been." Colleen started across the street.

Admittedly, Lucy had envisioned telling her sole girlfriend about her first sexual experience. Isn't that what women did? This, however, was not what she anticipated. As they walked to the market, Lucy could feel the tension building between her and Colleen. Was Colleen acting this way because she assumed Tony had talked about her?

Tony used a condom most of the time, but occasionally, like in Marge's bedroom, he forgot. Lucy had worried about getting pregnant but never considered venereal diseases or AIDs. As far as she could tell, Tony looked healthy. But then, she had nothing, no one, to compare him to. Maybe he wasn't supposed to swell that much.

"So you like him?" Colleen said.

"Of course. I wouldn't have otherwise."

"It's just that you're new at this and I worry, is all."

"There's no reason to worry. He's great to me," said Lucy.

As they turned on to Ninth Street, Lucy could smell fish. She smiled, reminded again how much she looked forward to Thursdays. The market was already crowded with an assortment of customers from the neighborhood, pecking through carts of produce. The two were jostled into the middle of the street by people walking with pizza slices, pork sandwiches, and water ice in hand. On either side were familiar storefronts with their aged, sunbleached awnings displaying family names. Metal stands huddled against the buildings bore everything from fruits and vegetables to sweat socks and bootleg movie videos.

Even though Lucy had spent most of her time here with Marge, the market always made her think of her father. Many of the stores were still Italian-owned and -run. Joseph was the one who was passionate about food, who taught Marge what she wanted to know. And then there were the snippets of Italian conversations wafting with the scents through the streets. It was music to Lucy, a long-forgotten, soothing lullaby from her father's lips. Marge had insisted that Joseph not speak Italian in front of the girls when they were children. She wanted her daughters to be entirely American. But Lucy would hear her father talking to his friends or the older neighbors outside, and she would sit next to him and listen.

Recently, Lucy found herself thinking about her father more and more. She wondered if, in some way, Tony reminded her of Joseph. Or maybe if she thought about Joseph, she didn't have to think about Marge. Her father had never forced her to do anything she didn't want to do. And she was certain that he would have loved her no matter what, he would never have betrayed her.

Colleen managed to work her way to one of the Korean vegetable stands. Lucy joined her, attracted by the red, green, and yellow peppers shimmering like bulbous jewels in the rough. Colleen picked up an eggplant that was so shiny and polished that Lucy could see her friend's scowl reflected in it.

"What?" Lucy asked.

"What nothing. You're happy. I'll keep my mouth shut."

"Just tell me what you want to tell me." Lucy wasn't interested in getting the silent treatment again, especially knowing that Colleen was withholding information or, at the very least, an adamant opinion. This woman offered the only other perspective on Lucy's life, on her world, save Jack's, and she couldn't talk to him about this. She was dependent on Colleen.

"If you're going to force me, fine. I suppose you should know what everyone else does. It's only fair." Colleen put the eggplant back in the bin and worked her way up the crowded sidewalk, calling behind her to Lucy. "There was this rumor in high school that Tony knocked up a girl. I won't say who."

Lucy, embarrassed, tried to put as little space as possible between the two. She didn't want people, even strangers, hearing tidbits about her boyfriend. Colleen stopped in front of the cheese shop. "Supposedly, she got an abortion and he didn't even help pay for it. I mean that's what they say."

Lucy's first thought was that the girl was her sister Anne. It didn't make sense, she knew, but Anne was the only one in high school that Lucy knew of who had supported abortion rights. She remembered Anne on television, the sun illuminating her golden hair, her patches of freckles. A high school boy's dream. Beautiful, athletic, and liberated. Lucy had always assumed that that meant her sister was having sex and possibly needed to have an abortion. Why else would Anne be so passionate about the issue, unless she needed one or thought she might need one down the line? But Anne and Tony had probably never met. She knew that Tony wasn't a virgin. She knew there'd been other women but she never imagined them pregnant. She never imagined Tony walking away from someone.

As Colleen opened the door, the old brass bell hanging from the top hinge rang. Lucy followed her. As usual there was a line; one of the owner's sons was passing out free samples to the customers. Lucy placed a chunk of Locatelli on her tongue and let it stick to the roof of her mouth like a Communion Host. She thought she heard Colleen humming. The market had always been Lucy's territory; she'd introduced it to Colleen. Now, she felt that it was being taken from her, as if her territory were being conquered and spoiled.

"You don't like it?" Colleen said nonchalantly.

"What?" asked Lucy, then realizing she was talking about the cheese, "No, I do. It's good."

"From the look on your face I thought you were going to toss it."

"I was thinking," Lucy said.

"Oh that. Don't worry about it. It was just a rumor. It probably isn't true. I mean you know the guy better than me, right? You know whether he would do something like that or not. And even if he did, he was just a kid."

Colleen ordered provolone, sliced thin, along with some shredded Parmesan. The silver blade hummed as it swayed back and forth cutting the provolone into nearly transparent slices. How odd, Lucy thought, that both Tony's and Colleen's stories were about unintended pregnancies, and which would be stranger — if both were lies or both were true?

Lucy mechanically recited her weekly order, temporarily halved after Marge's death, but recently restored with Tony's frequent presence at the dinner table. Why did happiness have to be so complicated? Sex was tainted with sin and the thought of Marge's watching. And now the possibility of love was tainted by Tony's reported past. Lucy wished for something simple in her life. Love like her father's. Love she could trust.

Chapter Fifteen

It was that time of year when everything from zero-down financing to heavy cream expired on June 30, Lucy's birthday. At the kitchen table, Lucy ran her fingers down the black-and-red newspaper pages searching for coupons to clip. There wasn't enough time; inevitably, she was going to miss a discount opportunity. Marge had taught her to be practical, to only clip the ones you needed, not the ones you thought you might want. But lately, Lucy felt that she had some catching up to do, even with the coupons. Next, she opened an envelope that had arrived in yesterday's mail; it was filled with menus and flyers offering limited-time special deals. Did Tony eat sushi? Would she? Did she need to lose weight? Get a tan? What about braces? She tapped her bottom and top teeth together, then pulled her lips back until she resembled a braying horse. The scissors slid off the table and clanked on the linoleum floor, bouncing once. Startled, Lucy jumped up from the chair, almost dancing around them.

She then heard Tony's voice from out front. Whenever she saw him she was positive that she loved him, but when he wasn't with her, she thought about Colleen's words. She pulled the front curtain aside and saw him standing with his back to the window, talking to someone in an idling SUV, which was wedged at a strange angle into the parking spot. Over his shoulder was the army duffle bag he'd inherited from one of his older brothers and used to carry his laundry.

It took her a moment to place the next voice she heard, since Tony's back blocked the driver from Lucy's view. It was Anne's voice. What was she doing here? Was her first instinct correct? Did they know each other after all? Anne climbed out of the car. Tony put his bag next to her on the sidewalk and got into the SUV. With arms folded across her chest, Anne looked up and down the block as though worried that someone would know she couldn't park her own car. Lucy wasn't sure what to do; maybe her sister wasn't coming to see her; maybe she was in the neighborhood for business and somehow had ended up parking in front of the house — the house that Anne had never been to before, talking to the boyfriend Anne had only spoken to once on the phone.

As Tony got out of the car and handed the keys to Anne, Lucy opened the front door and said, "Hey."

Anne and Tony bumped into each other as they approached her.

"Oh, you're coming to see Luce too?" Tony said.

Anne, looking disoriented, passed him and walked into the house. In the late afternoon light, Lucy could see that Anne had been crying and wondered how long she'd been trying to park her car. Tony followed Anne in, and they all stood in the relative darkness of the living room, the curtains drawn to keep the house cool. Tony's hands were shoved deep into his front pockets and he rocked slightly back and forth from toes to heels. The duffle bag still hung from his shoulder.

"I hope it's okay that I'm here," Anne said.

"Of course," Lucy said, although she was deeply confused. "This is Tony. This is my sister Anne."

"No kidding." Tony relieved himself of the duffle bag and shook Anne's hand. "Nice to meet you." Then, to Lucy, "I forgot you had a sister."

Lucy turned on one of the end table lamps and caught Anne's and Tony's reflections behind her own in the speckled mirror. For a moment, she imagined them embracing passionately, secretly, behind her back.

"Well, we haven't seen each other in a while," Anne said. They hadn't seen each other since Christmas dinner and hadn't spoken since Anne's odd and ill-timed phone call. Lucy had called her back and left several messages, but hadn't talked with her sister.

"This is a nice surprise," Lucy said.

"So, this is the new place?" Anne turned her face away from them and walked about the living room, gently touching dustless tabletops, careful not to disrupt the doilies. At their parents' black-and-white wedding photo taken outside St. Peter's, she stopped and traced the bottom edge with her index finger. A smile filled the bottom of their father's face, settling into his double chin; his eyes were squinted into half-moon slits against the bright afternoon sun. A curl from his thick windblown black hair had escaped and fallen onto his forehead. Beside his big frame, Marge looked tiny and particularly young, but neither naïve nor innocent. Despite being twenty years younger than her

husband, she in no way resembled a trophy wife; she was dressed conserva-
tively, wearing a high collar and white gloves and a stiff upper lip. Her face
seemed entirely resistant to the occasion and the sunlight. There was a slight
upward bend of her lips and her eyes stared straight ahead. Both seemed to
be looking to the future with trepidant courage.

"Well, this is a little more than freaky, Lucy." Anne sounded a little hoarse.
"This house is set up just like Mom's. It's like a museum in here. Did you
throw anything away?"

Lucy looked to Tony. She wanted him to disappear, or at least be stricken
deaf. Suddenly she was a child being reprimanded in front of her new and
untested best friend. He shrugged. He always said that he liked the house,
that it felt like home to him. Her hands reached to her forearms to tug on
the hair, but nothing was there.

"Except, of course, for that mirror. Please tell me that came with
the place."

Grateful for the change in topic, Lucy said, "Yeah, it was here when I
moved in."

When Jack came to finish the plasterwork in the front bedroom, they'd
talked about removing it. He'd also suggested painting the room, maybe
even relieving it of what he called the extraneous furnishings. That was the
day Jack and Tony met. Lucy had felt awkward introducing them. After Jack
headed home, Tony asked who he was. She explained he was just a friend,
really like a brother, although the description made her uneasy. That might
have been true before, and perhaps it was the fumes of home improvement,
but lately Lucy thought about him differently, thought about him kissing her.
Tony's reply had been, "I got brothers. None of them come over to fix stuff."
It wasn't until later, after dinner when they sat in the light of the television, cigarette smoke hovering between them, that Lucy thought that Tony
couldn't be truly jealous. Otherwise, he would have volunteered to help fix
up the house.

Anne stood behind Marge's recliner and stared down as if Marge was
there. Her manicured nails dug into the upholstery.

"Would you like to stay for dinner?" Lucy said.

Anne looked at Tony and then Lucy. "There was a fire at my house."

"Oh my God, are you okay?" Lucy said. "And Brad?"

"Yes, fine," she said. "Actually, Brad is out of the country on business.
I thought I'd stay with you for a while."

"Oh."

"Do you have a room I could stay in?"

"Sure."

"Thanks. Do you mind if I lie down for a little while? You know, smoke
inhalation and all that."

"Of course," Lucy said.

Anne turned to Tony and handed him her keys, "Would you mind bringing in my bags? I'd really appreciate it." She coughed the cough of one calling out sick.

Tony went to the car. As Lucy led Anne up the stairs, Anne muttered, "It continues." When she reached the bedroom door and saw her childhood room reassembled, she laughed. "I can't stay in here. This is too weird. And the wallpaper, it's psychedelic. Do you have another room?"

"No," said Lucy.

Anne backed out of the room. "Where do you sleep?" Lucy didn't respond. Anne walked to the front bedroom. "What exactly are you doing here, Lucy? Do you think she's coming back? That she'd be pissed if you didn't keep everything the way she had it?" Anne opened the closet door and saw that it was empty. "What did you do with her clothes?"

"I gave them away."

"I guess that's something. Anything else?" Anne said.

"No," Lucy said.

"I'll go through it all."

"There's nothing to go through," said Lucy.

Anne closed the closet door and opened a dresser drawer. "This is the woman who gave away your home. I don't understand why you would have any loyalty to her."

Her sister was acting just like Columbo — making conversation, picking up random items, until eventually he's handling the murder weapon. But Anne passed on touching the pillow. Nonetheless, Lucy felt like a suspect, as though everything was about to be taken from her.

"I don't understand why you're so angry. What do you care?" Lucy said.

"I'm just worried about you." Anne walked past Lucy and into the hall. "Don't worry I'll stay in the other room. This one's even scarier."

Anne plopped down on her pale yellow bedspread and threw herself back, stretching her hands above her head. "Is he your boyfriend?"

"I guess," Lucy said.

"Well, it's about time." Anne returned to a sitting position and ran her hands along the bed on either side of her. Her slightly swollen eyes noted every detail. "I'll be down in a little while."

Lucy left, thankful for the out. Immediately, she snuck into her room and hid the evidence-filled jewelry box in the bottom drawer of her dresser. She'd have to find a better place. Her sister was curious and might continue her house tour while Lucy was out.

Downstairs, Tony rested his head in his right hand, holding a cigarette. Smoke hung above his head like a thought balloon. He merely shook his head without raising it as he pointed to the large black canvas matching bags, all seven of them. "I'm not trying to say anything here. I don't know your sister. It's just seems like a lot to pack when you're running from a burning building."

Lucy sat next to him and stole his cigarette. As she took a deep drag, she was aware of her heart working to pump. She threw herself against the back of the plastic-covered couch and exhaled. Despite the dryness in her mouth, she took another drag. Tony leaned back, took her unoccupied hand, and kissed her on the lips. The kiss. The kiss that meant the procedure had begun; sex was inevitable. A formality much like a handshake at introduction.

"I'm sorry, Tony," Lucy sat up and leaned over the ashtray, pointing upstairs with the cigarette.

"The stuff doesn't even smell like smoke," he said. Everyone was a detective.

"I think I should talk to her."

"Sounds like a good idea." He took the cigarette back. "You want me to leave?"

"Would that be okay?"

"Sure," he paused, "Can I come by tomorrow?"

"I'm not sure what's going on," Lucy said, and then realized he was looking at his laundry bag. "Afternoon, okay?"

"Thanks, Luce. You're the best." He kissed the top of her head.

*   *   *

Standing in the basement, as far away from her sister as she could within the house, Lucy could still feel the presence of another human being. The house felt crowded. The cement floor and low exposed ceiling beams of the damp basement sandwiched her as the piles of sorted laundry grew around her like colorful shrubbery. Lucy was accustomed to her mother's presence, real or imagined, to the sensation of being watched, judged. With Anne, she could be exposed in her new life as the Lucy of the old life, exposed as a murderer, or worse, as an isolated, almost thirty-year-old freak of society.

Tony left his socks in knotted balls. He forgot to take paper and change out of his pockets. At certain times, such as when Lucy was sorting his laundry or cooking him one of his favorite meals or cleaning the dishes as he retired to the living room, she thought of that first night when they had shared cappuccinos and she wondered if she'd passed a domesticity test. She put this out of her mind once again and returned to the problem of her sister. Marge wouldn't have tolerated this. Marge wouldn't have tolerated Anne inviting herself to stay. Marge wouldn't have tolerated Anne lying. Lucy grew angry at Tony's clothes, banging his socks against the dryer until they unrolled, yanking his pant legs inside out. She took a deep breath and tried to convince herself that she wasn't angry with him or his clothes but with Anne for ruining their evening, for intruding on their life.

What was it to Anne if she had a boyfriend? Her sister had said the word with such condescension, as if Lucy had conjured an imaginary friend to take responsibility for wetting the bed. At times, Anne was Marge. Anne's first boyfriend, at least the one the family knew about, was Robert. He was tall, yet he hadn't quite grown into his hands or feet. His face, too, while in better shape than most boys' faces, needed to grow around his nose. Despite this, he was attractive. He attended the brother school of their high school, and the two had met at a track meet. Anne brought him in the house one afternoon, sat him at the kitchen table, and fixed lunch. He ate three turkey sandwiches and guzzled four glasses of milk. Lucy quietly watched, impressed by the skinny boy's capacity. When Marge, who had been at Mrs. Garrity's, entered the room, it became as tense as if she had discovered them fornicating on the formica. She ignored the boy and said to Anne, "Clean up after yourself," and left. Brad, years later, was the only other boy-friend to come into the Pescitelli household.

When Lucy returned from starting Tony's laundry in the basement, Anne was standing by the stove. The kettle was about to boil. From her mug, the tag of an unfamiliar tea bag hung over the side.

"I knew to bring my own this time," said Anne.

Lucy took her place at the table and lit a cigarette, pondering just how much time her sister did have to pack.

"What did Mom send you?" Lucy asked.

"That woman is crazy. Was crazy," said Anne, as she poured the boiling water into her mug, turning her face from the steam's funnel.

Lucy wondered when their mother became "that woman" to Anne.

"She had your lawyer friend send me a certified letter six months to the date after her death. Even in death, she thinks she's in some detective movie of the week."

"What did it say?" The storyline was familiar to Lucy. Was it Matlock? Some horrifying family secret was revealed; the result was murder.

Anne scooped up her teabag with the spoon. "Well, turns out that Dad isn't my dad." She squished her thumb into the teabag until it began to tear; dark fluid dripped into the mug.

"What are you talking about? Of course he is."

"No. Apparently, he's not. Don't worry; he's still your dad." She joined her sister at the table, held the cup under her nose, and inhaled deeply. "He married Mom because she was pregnant with me by some other guy."

Lucy's skin heated as if she was the one who'd lied. "That's impossible. Mom pregnant? No way," she said.

"Hey, this is what she wrote. I'm not making it up," Anne said.

"I'm not saying you are. It's just hard to believe, knowing Mom and all. Can I see the letter?"

"I don't have it with me."

Lucy was suspicious that her sister forgot to pack something of such im-portance. "Are you sure Dad knew?"

"That's what she said. He knew all along."

Lucy wanted to feel compassion for her sister, to believe her, but she had to admit that her first thought when Anne said she needed a place to stay is that her sister never would have shown up if Marge were alive, if it was Marge's house. It would have been admitting defeat. Somehow it was fine to show up on her doorstep, demanding a place to stay, telling wild stories.

"Are you sure she was telling the truth?" Lucy felt uncomfortable asking this question. When it came to Anne, she had always sided with her mother. It was an unacknowledged habit, more ingrained then pulling on her forearm hair. However, since her mother's death, Lucy knew Marge kept secrets, maybe even lied.

"I think so. I mean, if you think about it, I never fit in here. I'm nothing like Dad. Your dad." Anne looked into her cup as if the answers lay in floating escaped tea leaves. "Maybe it's why Mom always hated me."

"Mom didn't hate you."

Anne cocked her head to the side. "Yeah, it was a real love relationship."

"And Dad loved you."

"That was just the way he was."

"You only remember the bad," said Lucy.

"Can you remember the good?" her sister said, "Name one happy memory with Mom. One time we were all laughing, or a time when she just hugged us out of nowhere. One thing we looked forward to like any normal family — like the holidays or vacation. Every day was just something to be lived through for Mom. And she made it that way for us too."

They sat with their respective drinks. Lucy put coupons into stacks as Marge had done, by type of product in order of expiration date. Anne stirred her tea, watching her sister perform a ritual that must have been lodged deep in her childhood memories.

Lucy knew that Anne's childhood was different from hers. There are siblings who confuse their memories, what happened to whom, who did what first, their childhoods practically interchangeable. Not so with Lucy and Anne. It was as if they grew up in two separate households. One had an affectionate, funny father and a practical mother; the other had a silly father and a demonic mother. Now, it seemed to Lucy that her father had tried too hard to love his daughters the same. As if he kept a checklist in his head making sure the score was even, that whatever he'd given to one, he'd given to the other. Each night, when he came home from work, he would insist on hugs from his daughters before entering the kitchen to have Marge swat him away with a spoon or spatula. Lucy always ran to him; it was her favorite moment of the day. Sometimes he would kiddingly chase Anne around the dining room table until he caught her, hugging her, then tickling her. Anne would pry herself loose and run upstairs. But he loved Anne. It wasn't a game. And if this was true, that Anne's father was a stranger, didn't it make

Joseph's love even more precious?

"You're being unfair. Mom loved us. Mom loved you. In her way," Lucy said. "She never beat us."

"Well, give her an award already," Anne said. "It doesn't matter now. She's dead. We'll never figure her out."

"Did she tell who your dad was?"

"Yeah, some doctor guy."

"Are you going to contact him?"

"And say what? I'm sure he'll want nothing to do with me."

"You don't know that." Lucy, finished with the coupons, rubbed her forearms.

"What would be the point anyway? I'm a grown woman. What do I need a father for?" Anne watched Lucy as she sipped from the cup, then pointed to her own face and said, "What happened to your hair?"

"Waxed it."

"Huh," Anne said.

Lucy reached for her cigarette box and quickly changed the subject. "Do you think Dad loved Mom?"

"Your dad?"

Lucy nodded. "He stayed with her 'til he died."

"He was in love with someone else. You know — a love that dare not speak its name."

Lucy stared at her sister.

"Dad was gay," Anne said.

"That's ridiculous," she said, staring at her sister. Over the past few months, she had grown used to being suspicious of her mother but she refused to question the memory of her father. "Isn't your news crazy enough? Do you really have to invent stuff?"

"Really. Why else would he have married her and stayed with her?" Anne smirked, then waved her hand in the air. "Forget it. I was kidding."

They sat silently, clutching their cups, sipping. Her sister could say such hateful things. Lucy knew she had the right to be angry, but did she have to deny their mother Joseph's love? She could hear Tony's clothes in the final spin cycle, clinging to the side of the washer. How many times had Marge sat at this table, drinking coffee and smoking, waiting to change over laundry? She took care of Joseph and would have for many more years, without complaint, if he hadn't died that day at the site. The washer came to a slow rattling stop and Lucy left her sister in the kitchen.

Chapter Sixteen

Lucy woke up alone in bed, a rarity on the weekend. Tony's parents were in town so he was at home. Tonight, Lucy was to meet them for the first time. They'd come up especially for her thirtieth birthday, and the four of them were going to dinner to celebrate. Tony had told her not to be nervous, that just hearing about her, his parents loved her already. But Lucy couldn't help but worry; she'd never been in this situation before and wasn't sure how to act.

Lucy closed her eyes and imagined Tony still asleep in his parents' house, in his childhood bedroom, in the same single bed he'd slept in since he'd graduated from his crib. Of course, she had never been in his house, so she wasn't sure from where she was conjuring these peaceful, sun-filled images — the wooden red, white, and blue sailboat lamp on his bedside table and the Little League trophies on his bureau. In her imagination, Tony, glowing in the natural light, awoke without his morning beard, without sleep in his eyes. He rolled over and smiled at her as though he were a movie star manipulating the audience with a calculated sexy expression aimed directly into the camera. It worked; Lucy felt flushed.

She rolled over and placed her hand where his head usually rested. Her movement made her aware of her legs, silky and hairless, against the soft sheets, and her breasts against Tony's threadbare Temple T-shirt. In her mind, Tony's skin was smooth and cool as she pressed herself against him. He smelt of clean laundry.

"Lucy!" Anne called from the kitchen, through the bedroom floor. "Where's the skim milk?" She'd been there for over a week.

A moment later, the Delvecchio sisters responded to Anne's loud whine by pounding on their respective kitchen walls.

Skim milk was not a staple in Lucy's refrigerator, since she didn't drink it.

"Lucy!" Anne shouted again, followed by more banging and muffled complaints from the neighbors.

Lucy pulled herself from her soft cocoon and trudged to the top of the stairs. "I'll go to the store."

When she arrived in the kitchen, Anne, in her newly adopted daily uniform of a green flannel robe, was writing a grocery list.

"There's nothing to eat in this house," Anne said. She'd pulled an index card from the drawer. Apparently, she remembered where some things were kept.

"What do you want? I can make you something," Lucy offered as she poured herself a glass of orange juice. There'd be time for coffee when she got back.

"I'll make some toast while you're gone, I guess." Anne stood as she handed Lucy the card.

The supermarket was crowded with weekend shoppers. One of the advantages Lucy enjoyed by working nights was free run of the aisles during the weekdays. With Anne's list of odd requests in hand, Lucy was forced to travel up and down the aisles searching for unfamiliar products, such as kiwis, rice cakes, pita bread and hummus. They didn't print coupons for these items.

At least Lucy left the house without fear of Anne discovering her jewelry box filled with incriminating evidence and morbid keepsakes. In the past week, Anne, through her words and actions, showed no interest in uncovering Lucy's crime. Anne didn't suspect her, found her utterly not compelling, and to Lucy this felt like an insult. Lucy was certain she could leave a diary open on the kitchen table and Anne, after glancing at the rounded scribble and recognizing it as her sister's, would push it aside, choosing to read once again about the dietary benefits of the oriental ingredients of her tea rather than learn her sister's deepest, darkest, movie-of-the-week-worthy secrets. Her sister assumed she had none. At times, Lucy wanted to shout, "I killed her!" just to get the credit, just to be seen as interesting.

As Lucy turned onto aisle three — Household Cleaners, Pesticides, and Feminine Hygiene — her cart caught the corner of a box and a tower of cardboard teetered. At first she thought she'd hit a clerk. She managed to save the pile, with the exception of the top box, which she caught in her arms. No one was injured. Surprisingly, no one saw.

Kotex. The boxes read Kotex. And suddenly, Lucy couldn't remember when she'd had her last period. Sex in her mother's bed came to her mind immediately; that day kept coming up and she never felt good about it. Holding the maxi pad box against her chest, she wondered if she could be pregnant. Her mind was at a standstill. This was a new worry. Her cycle had been normal; she always sensed its arrival, and so she never kept track of it like the women in movies did, marking large red *X*s on their calendars. Mindlessly, she tossed the box into the cart and moved down the aisle. Tony and she had been dating for a few months. She recalled having at least one period, because she remembered telling Tony that she had a headache. He seemed to understand, saying, "Let me know when you're done."

The long lines of shopping carts at the counters resembled free-floating octopus tentacles. For a few minutes, Lucy couldn't decipher the end of any line. Finally she pulled up behind a woman with two overflowing carts; one she pushed in front of her and the other she pulled behind her. Lucy counted three young boys who kept bringing sugary or salty snacks to her, hoping to get something in the cart at the last minute after breaking her down throughout the excursion. It was then that Lucy remembered the skim milk. She told the man behind her that she would be right back and raced down the refrigerated aisle. She always saved the cold stuff for last, no matter what the weather, but she was terribly distracted. When she returned, the man had not saved her place, and her cart was in line limbo, lost in the maze.

At last, Lucy reached a checkout and placed her items on the conveyer belt by weight and type, kiwis last. She hoped that they were ripe; Anne hadn't provided any instructions.

"Coupons?" asked the cashier.

"Not today," Lucy said as she bagged the groceries. Marge had never allowed the clerks to bag, complaining that they would put cleaners in with produce and never wrap the meats with an extra plastic bag. Lucy recalled one summer afternoon during high school when Mary, a girl in her class, was working as a bagger. Marge had yelled at the girl the moment she noisily opened a brown paper bag, "Oh no you don't. She'll pack," pointing to Lucy. "If anyone's going to poison my family, it'll be her." Lucy, feeling the heat of embarrassment rise from her chest to her ears, had sorted and wrapped and packed, while Mary's expression clearly said, "Whatever;" Marge had smugly looked on as if she'd rallied an important cause.

While the cashier, pleasant but slow-moving, counted kiwis, Lucy reviewed Anne's grocery list, the cursive writing drawn in dull pencil. After all the trouble, her sister had forgotten the skim milk too. A laugh rose from Lucy, and the clerk asked her, "What?"

"Nothing," Lucy said.

The Donatos weren't expecting to meet the mother of their grandchild tonight. Lucy could feel her stomach manufacturing acid; she couldn't imagine sitting across the table from Tony's mother, passing the breadbasket and butter, and thinking there was a child in her belly. She had to know if she was pregnant. They'd been careful, mostly. She tried to account for periods, but decided she needed to purchase a pregnancy test. Where could she buy it without running into anyone? Where would she take it? She missed having the house to herself; her freedom was too short-lived. Then there was eternal damnation. Sex outside of marriage. Birth control. Did using a pregnancy test outside of marriage count as a sin too? She was just getting deeper and deeper into trouble. If she could just get through today, if she just wasn't pregnant, if Tony's parents could just love her, then she'd never sin again. Maybe she'd even work up the courage to go to confession.

The Delvecchio sisters loitered in their lawn chairs and merely stared at Lucy, even after she mumbled a "Morning." Their silence made her even more uncomfortable than their usual talk did. Lucy imagined that they knew what she was worried about, they'd been expecting it, hoping for it, so they could argue with each other.

"I told you so. Just a matter of time."

"No, I told you."

However, they couldn't hold their silence. As Lucy opened her door, the one on the right said, "Tell that sister of yours to keep it down. What is she? Three years old?"

From the left, "Some people's children."

Lucy closed the door behind her and wondered how they knew that Anne was her sister, considering the lack of family resemblance. The Delvecchios, on the other hand, could be spotted as sisters a block away. Did they sit perched on kitchen chairs, ears suctioned to highball glasses pressed against the wall, listening to Lucy and Anne talk, to Lucy and Tony make love? She was grateful that they hadn't lived next to Marge; surely they would have turned Lucy in to the authorities.

Anne was sprawled on the sofa under her bedspread, watching a talk show in which people were being reunited with their birth mothers. Two heavyset women, mother and daughter, with almost identically dyed orange-yellow hair, hugged each other as the host dabbed her eyes with a tissue and the audience clapped.

"You don't know how lucky you are. I wish I was put up for adoption," Anne said to the television.

"I got your stuff. You know, you forgot to put milk on the list," Lucy said. At times, she missed the old version of her sister, as opinionated as she was, she never felt sorry for herself. Anne had been self-reliant and energetic. Lucy couldn't remember Anne spending any time in the living room, Marge's stronghold, let alone staring at the television for any length of time, or talking to it. Now, if Anne wasn't lounging on the couch, she was sleeping in bed. Her sister seemed depressed and Lucy wondered if a lot of television viewing was a sign of depression or if watching a lot of television made you depressed. Marge watched TV every night.

"Did I?" Anne pushed against a couch cushion making it crinkle. "Lucy, when are you going to take off these plastic covers?"

"Have you been talking to the neighbors?" Lucy said.

"No."

"Do you want any of this now?" Lucy swung the bags in front of the TV.

"No thanks."

Anne's behavior didn't seem to coincide with the revelation of her paternity. Her sister should have been angry, enraged, throwing things, cursing Marge. Something else was going on, and Lucy didn't buy the fire story. She decided she'd follow up on it, but after she had dealt with her own crisis. Now she was playing detective. As Lucy put the groceries away, she planned her pregnancy test excursion. She'd take a bus into Center City; no one knew her there, and no one she knew went there. In an anonymous pharmacy, she'd make her purchase. When she got home, she hoped Anne would be napping. She took a token from her purse and held it in her fist, ready to sight the first bus. She hoisted her purse onto her shoulder and quickly headed for the front door.

"Where you going?" Anne said.

"Out." Lucy caught herself sounding like Anne the teenager.

"Can you bring me some ginger ale?"

"They sell it on the corner."

"Please, Lucy."

"I'll try to remember," Lucy said. Who the hell was this person? Lucy was used to caring for someone else. Toward the end of her mother's life she did everything, even if it was under Marge's scrutiny. But Marge never seemed needy or dependent. It wasn't in her. And Lucy never thought it was in Anne. What did she know? She hadn't lived with Anne in almost fifteen years. Maybe her sister wasn't the same person. Lucy had stayed the same, only the last six months had changed her. Did Anne notice a difference in her?

The Delvecchio sisters were absent from their posts, perhaps allowing for a bathroom break, so Lucy took advantage by briskly walking down the street. She turned on the northbound street, and seeing a bus, ran for the corner. As she boarded, she quickly scanned the street to make sure no one had seen her, thinking she should be worried about what to wear to dinner, not about whether she was creating the next generation of Donatos. No one she knew was on the bus. It wasn't until she sat behind the driver that she considered that this could be Glenn Lepper's route and she'd need to be more careful on the way back. The bus passed several corners, since no one was waiting to get on and no one had requested a stop. When it did stop, the brakes shrieked, adding to Lucy's tension and, she had to admit, her excitement.

Something was happening to her, something of her own making. She hadn't intended to get pregnant, but now she found herself in a real situation, possibly, and it was exciting. Her mother's strange enthusiasm came to mind. When Marge got cancer, she ardently immersed herself in planning her death, claiming the remainder of her life. The exhilaration of making the unknown yours, now this was Lucy's alone, at least as she sat on the bus.

The lurching of the bus kept her aware of her movement through the city. She didn't have a particular destination in mind, but she knew it had to be far enough away. What would she do if it were true? She'd have to tell Tony. Would he marry her, as her father had married her mother? What had been Marge's options? Lucy didn't know her mother's family, but she was certain that there wasn't an aunt living somewhere in the Midwest to ship Marge off to. She'd been disowned by her family for marrying Joseph, a Catholic, an Italian. What if they knew that she was carrying an illegitimate child, someone else's child? For the first time, Lucy realized that maybe her mother had lied to her about why her family didn't speak to her. What would Marge have done if Joseph hadn't married her?

Lucy rode past block after block of row houses, some three-story, some two-story, and in varying conditions. The sky was cloudless and flat, so that when she reached Society Hill, with its bright brick and authentic colonial colors, she felt like she was on a film set and the house fronts were propped up with wood scaffolding. When Independence Hall came into view, Lucy pulled the cord to request a stop. In grade school, they'd visited the Liberty Bell on a school trip once, so she was somewhat familiar with the area. Chestnut Street looked promising in her search for a pharmacy.

A few blocks west, she saw a small one, probably family run, squished between a dollar store and a print shop. The peeling sign out front read, *Since 1932*. A bell sounded softly as she opened the door. The store was dimly lit and, except for the pharmacy sign hanging in the back, she would have mistaken it for a souvenir shop — racks of postcards of the Liberty Bell, Independence Hall, The Philadelphia Art Museum (with and without Rocky Balboa triumphantly jumping), and the city's skyline at various times of day. Miniature Liberty Bells in a multitude of sizes sat on the counter top next to the door. Beside them stacks of T-shirts and small soft pretzel pins. A thin layer of dust covered everything.

"Be right with ya," said a man's voice from the back.

Following the voice, Lucy discovered a shelf holding a plethora of pregnancy tests; she hadn't realized there would be so many. What should she consider? All of them said they were the most accurate. One box had two tests inside and she decided this would be best. Despite their claims of accuracy, she wanted to be extra certain either way.

"What can I do ya for?" An older gentlemen in a white jacket emerged from behind the pharmacy counter, bifocal glasses perched on his nose.

"I just need a few things." Lucy grabbed another test, a different brand, and then moved down the aisle looking for something else to purchase. Bags of candies hung from hooks. Lucy figured the hard candies would be the safest; the chocolates were probably stale. Quickly she moved to the counter and dumped her boxes and bags. "That's it." From the depths of her purse, she searched for her wallet and avoided eye contact with the pharmacist.

"That'll be fifty-three twenty-six," he said as he slowly lifted each item and placed them in a thin, practically see-through bag.

The amount surprised Lucy; she hadn't considered cost, but she stopped herself from protesting and handed over sixty dollars.

The pharmacist peered over his glasses as he handed her the bag.

"For a friend of yours, right?" he said as he winked.

Lucy grabbed the bag, held out her hand for the change then abruptly turned and scurried out. A boarded-up, one-screen movie theatre a few doors down provided a private alcove for her to transfer the pregnancy tests from the plastic bag to her purse. The candy would be a decoy if she ran into anyone or if Glenn was driving the bus. She would explain that she was picking up some candies for the funeral home.

On the return trip home, she was plagued with many of the same thoughts as on the way to the pharmacy. A new one emerged to preoccupy Lucy as she neared home — the thought that she could be living her mother's life over again, that she could find herself pregnant and rejected by the father. The idea of her mother being frightened was foreign to Lucy, but Marge must have been, especially in the sixties and coming from a strict family. Joseph had saved her though, given her a home and continued respectability. Marge must have loved him for that, loved him despite their differences, despite his optimism and relentless joy. Then, the strangest thought came to Lucy. Tony wouldn't marry her, just like in Colleen's story, but Jack would. Jack would give her all the things her father had tried to give Marge. This comforted Lucy and she let herself relax into the hard plastic seat, let the bus sway her, and saw Jack tossing a ball out front to the kids in the street and herself on the stoop, cradling her swollen belly. The bus passed her street and Lucy jumped out of her seat and called to the bus driver to stop. She physically shook the vision of Jack out of her head as she walked down the street.

The sidewalk was still Delvecchio-free as Lucy cautiously entered the house, gently pulling the screen door closed. Anne had left the couch. At the top of the stairs, Lucy tiptoed to Anne's bedroom door and gently pressed her ear against it. Quiet. Suddenly she felt like her spying neighbors. She went into the bathroom and placed her purse and the bag filled with candy on the floor. As quietly as possible, she closed and locked the door, then removed the tests from her purse. Each was wrapped in cellophane, very noisy, which caused Lucy to pause. After she turned the shower, she ripped off the wrappings. Adding to the urgency of the situation, she realized her bladder was full. With one hand she pulled down her pants, with the other she shook open the instruction for the package that contained the two tests. She sat and read quickly, bouncing her knees. After pulling the lids off both tests, she peed on the exposed sticks and recapped them. She held the rest of her urine for the third test, which she opened immediately. Once her bladder was empty, she realized that she had no way of timing the tests. She didn't wear a watch. Her days revolved around tasks, not clocks. She was scared. She was nervous. She was tremendously alive. Sitting on the toilet, she took a cigarette from her purse. The last time she'd smoked in the bathroom had been that day with rose petals under her feet.

One-one thousand, two-one thousand, she began. Between numbers, she tried to recall her co-worker Ralph talking about his wife and the things she did when she was pregnant. According to him, his wife either wanted to eat everything, peculiar things, or nothing at all. He worried that she'd forget to dress the kids for school and then send them off without lunches. The house was a disaster area because her energy level plummeted. Twenty-two-one thousand. Lucy ate what she normally ate. The house was immaculate as usual, even with the addition of the lethargic Anne. Lucy had to admit she was tired more often, but with Tony staying over, there was reason to stay up late. Sex was exercise. She had to admit that as her only form of cardiovascular activity, it wore her out. Thirty-six-one thousand. Why couldn't she remember her periods? Maybe she was pregnant, if she was forgetting them.

"Lucy." Anne banged on the door.

Lucy jumped up, tossed her cigarette in the bowl, and stumbled to the door with her pants still around her ankles. The ginger ale — she'd forgotten.

"Yeah?" Lucy waved the smoke around.

"I need the bathroom . . . now."

"Be right out." Lucy kicked off her pants as she pulled her shirt over her head. The shower water was cold. She twisted on the hot water tap and climbed in the tub hoping it would kick in soon. Anne continued knocking on the door. Lucy splashed the water on her body and hair since it was still too cold to stand under. She turned off the shower, wrapped a towel around herself, and flushed the toilet.

"What are you doing?"

"Coming." Lucy tossed the tests and their packaging into her purse, picked up the candy bag, and bundled her clothes in her arms.

"I'm out," she said to Anne as she opened the door.

Her sister pushed past her and slammed the door shut.

It was an early dinner with Tony's parents. Lucy needed to start getting ready soon. She tossed her clothes on the floor and took the tests from her bag. Each one she placed carefully on top of the cardboard box it had come in. All of them read negative. Despite not having a start time, she checked the clock. She sat on the bed facing the dresser. Water dripped from her hair and ran down her spine; she wriggled each time it startled her. She would wait another three minutes, just in case. The clock was an old manual one and its ticking was audible. The sound would have driven anyone unaccustomed to it crazy, but Lucy gently swayed back and forth to the ticking, as if she were a metronome, rubbing her forearms and staring at her reflection in the dresser mirror. The dresser stood where the alcove had been in her old bedroom. She no longer imagined visitations from the Blessed Virgin or the Saints, instead she saw herself. How her appearance had changed over the years. She'd been looking at herself with the same wooden frame around her forever. She was no longer a child, an innocent. And she wasn't just Marge's younger daughter. She was a woman, who had killed, who had a lover, who might have been a mother. Paranoia, she thought, now able to think clearly. With Tony's story about Colleen and Colleen's about Tony, all these tales of unwanted pregnancy, no wonder it was her conclusion. She had none of the symptoms of pregnancy. The tests were negative. She looked up and watched herself softly laugh in the mirror as if she was counseling someone else. What a fool you've been!

The bathroom door squeaked open and the toilet bowl gurgled as it filled up, then Anne's door shut. Lucy tossed the tests into the shopping bag with the candy and pushed them to the bottom of her trashcan. She stood too quickly and felt lightheaded. Spots appeared before her eyes. A moment of clarity came to her — Anne was tired, Anne was forgetful, Anne was eating strange things. Anne was pregnant. Lucy tightened the towel around her chest and went to knock on Anne's door but stood there quietly instead, not knowing what to say.

Chapter Seventeen

When the Donatos came to pick up Lucy, Tony was sitting in the front passenger seat next to his father, so Lucy joined Mrs. Donato in the back seat. Tony's mother placed her hands on either side of Lucy's face and enthusiastically kissed her on the cheek before Lucy had even closed the door. When Mrs. Donato pulled back from Lucy, her hands remained and she turned Lucy's face delicately from side to side as if considering purchasing a serving dish. The close inspection made Lucy glad that she'd ignored the Stardust system's instructions and waxed prematurely.

"Adorable, just adorable," Mrs. Donato proclaimed.

Through this simple, brief exchange, Lucy understood that Tony's mother in no way resembled her own. Marge bestowed dry pecks, with just a dusting of lipstick, near the cheeks of widows and brides on those momentous occasions, as though she only had so many to give in a lifetime. Mrs. Donato's makeup was beautifully applied in a fashion she must have practiced for years. She smelt of dried roses.

At the stop sign, Mr. Donato reached his right hand over the high seat back. "Miss Pescitelli, a pleasure," he said.

Lucy shook his hand. He wore a beige duff cap that covered his thick white hair, and a pale blue jacket. Lucy could see what Tony would look like at that age. His hand returned a moment later waving a thin, white handkerchief as if in surrender.

"Looks like she got ya," he said.

"Oh, goodness. Sorry." Mrs. Donato snatched the hankie and rubbed Lucy's cheek. Lucy tried not to flinch at the sudden unexpected contact.

The four arrived at the restaurant. It was a large, corner row house that Lucy had passed many times since her move but had never been inside. Tony always said he preferred her home cooking to any restaurant's food, so they didn't eat out. There were pillars in the entranceway and a fresco of a vineyard along one of the walls. The maître d' led them to a table next to the stone fireplace ablaze with candles, but Mrs. Donato, grasping Lucy's arm, insisted that they be seated in front by the bay window.

"One of the advantages of getting here early," she said.

They arrived at the table and Mrs. Donato let go of Lucy's arm, but not before patting it.

"Such lovely skin," she said.

Once seated, Mr. Donato requested a bottle of champagne. His hand rested on his wife's knee. If her father were alive, she thought, he and Mr. Donato would have given each other big manly hugs. (Manly hugs, she repeated to herself.) He would have kissed Mrs. Donato before she'd been able to kiss him. The thought of reaching out and holding Tony's hand occurred to her, but he was preoccupied, pulling bread apart and digging for butter in the bottom of the basket. With them, this family, she was acutely aware of being more Marge's daughter than Joseph's.

"We've got big news tonight," said Mr. Donato.

Tony threw his arm over the back of Lucy's chair. One of his cheeks was filled with half a dinner roll.

"Don't fill up on bread," his mother said. On the front of her pale pink shirt was an ocean scene.

As usual, Lucy wore black (somewhat faded from washings). Most of her outfits were black so that she could wear them "out," or wear them to work, and look appropriate in either place. But for the most part, work had been the only "out" for her. Since she started at Botti's, since her father died, since high school, she'd been wearing black.

Once the champagne was poured, Mr. Donato raised his flute and said, "To Lucy. Happy birthday!" All the flutes met in the center of the table as Tony and Mrs. Donato wished her happy birthday, too.

With his glass still in hand, Mr. Donato began to speak, gesturing with his hands. The champagne swayed back and forth, almost sloshing over the edge. "Now that we know that Tony's in good hands, Lucy, we're moving to Jersey for good and selling the house here." He lifted his glass again, "To new beginnings." Mrs. Donato, Tony, and Lucy gently clanked their glasses to his and softly repeated, "To new beginnings." Lucy saw Mrs. Donato wink at Tony.

"Congratulations," Lucy said. In unison, the Donatos replied, "Thank you." Tony didn't seem surprised by the news and Lucy wondered if this presentation was exclusively for her benefit.

"Let's order some grub, huh?" Tony opened his menu so as to block his parents' view and leaned over to place a kiss on Lucy's cheek, all the while avoiding eye contact with her.

"You can't fool us," Mrs. Donato said as she tugged playfully at the menu, then laughed a little too long. "We know you two are smitten."

Mr. Donato grabbed his son's neck and patted him heavily on the back. Lucy merely smiled and nodded. Tony kept his eyes on the menu as he attempted to smother a grin. Little sweat beads formed around the edge of his hairline.

The waiter returned and Mr. Donato ordered for the family. The topic of selling the house was set aside as though all decisions had been made and all discussions exhausted. Tony approached his dinner slowly, lacking his usual gusto. He twirled his pasta too many times and held his bread too long in the sauce until it was soggy. Lucy, too, was eating carefully, trying not to drop food in her lap or speak with her mouth full. His parents ate and spoke in turns.

"Tony told us you took care of your mother right up 'til the end. At home. That's really wonderful," said his mother.

"Thank you," Lucy said.

"Selflessness is a lost art. It used to be something women were good at, wanted to be good at," his mother continued.

"It's a woman at her best," his father chimed in.

"It's just wonderful to know that our Tony has found a woman who respects family. Not some career gal who's gonna let strangers raise her kids, who dumps her parents in an old people's home." Mrs. Donato took her mauve napkin from her lap and shook out the crumbs like a matador taunting a bull with his cape. "I don't mind telling you, my daughter-in-laws — of course, don't tell my sons this — are no great catches. My sons would have been better off bachelors, taking care of themselves."

Mr. Donato gave his wife a look that she must have recognized.

"Well, this night isn't about them," she said raising her glass. "To Lucy. Happy birthday."

"Thank you. You're very sweet," said Lucy after quickly swallowing the last of her veal scaloppini. A bus boy came to clear their dinner plates, and Lucy was relieved to see this signal that the evening was progressing. There would be an end. Something wasn't being said. This was something Lucy could now recognize from her own family. The table was cleared and they sat silently for a moment, waiting for the dessert cart to be wheeled to them. Mrs. Donato cleared her throat and kicked her son under the table, startling Lucy. Tony peeked at his mother and then for the first time in the evening looked directly into Lucy's eyes. She busied herself by folding her napkin into threes. This time Tony cleared his throat to get Lucy's attention.

He pulled a ring box from his pants pocket and said, "It's like my parents were saying Luce, you're very special."

Tony's parents sat stiffly, eyebrows raised, smiles so large but somehow tentative, they resembled frightened clowns. Tony held the box open, a gold ring with a single modest diamond shown with the light of the streetlamp outside.

"Luce . . . "

"Ah, Tony?" His mother said under her breath and nodded toward the floor. Tony slid his chair back and knelt on one knee.

"Luce. Would you do me the honor of being my wife and the mother of my children?"

"Tony, I . . . ," Lucy began.

"It's all true. You're selfless and wonderful and . . . " he said. Now he lifted his face toward her. On his knee, next to his parents, he seemed so young to Lucy, so vulnerable, she wanted to hold him, protect him. His parents remained frozen in expectant joy. For the first time, she recognized the presence of the other patrons in the restaurant. They too waited, some burdened with food-filled utensils hanging in midair. She understood the secret now. How could she not have guessed? Why had she assumed the worst?

She felt pulled into an intense undertow. Her father always told her not to fight it, to let the water take her, then when the water released its grip, to swim. She swayed, took a deep breath.

"I've waited a long time to find a woman as good as my mother, " he said.

The answer was yes, Lucy knew, but she couldn't say it. Of course, it was yes. She'd had sex with him. This afternoon she thought she might have been pregnant. And she loved him, she had to love him; they'd had sex.

"Yes, I'll marry you."

His parents leapt from their chairs, jostling the table. The flutes clanked of their own accord, champagne snuffing out the tumbled candles. Tony struggled to get off his knees and embrace his fiancée before his parents did. The four hugged and the other patrons cheered, clapped, and raised their glasses. It felt like a movie to Lucy as the maître d' presented another bottle of champagne and a platter of strawberries and chocolates, while a troop of bus boys tidied the table. It was then that Mrs. Donato admitted, "This is where Al proposed to me forty-six years ago."

Since the death of her father, nothing of consequence had happened to Lucy until these past months — her mother's death and her role in that, moving out of the house she'd lived in all her life, and losing her virginity. And then, in just this one day, a pregnancy scare and an unrelated proposal of marriage. Had the pacing of her life changed for good? Would any of this have happened without Marge's death? At thirty, forty, fifty, would she still have lived with her mother, worked at the funeral home, and stayed the same?

"I'm so happy," said his mother once they were seated and the ring had been placed on Lucy's finger. "I always wanted a daughter, you know. And don't worry about the wedding, dear. We'll pay for everything. I've got it all figured out. I'll make sure it's just what your mother would have wanted."

Through dessert, Mrs. Donato continued talking in detail about caterers and deejays and invitations and bridesmaids. There would need to be at least three, since Tony had three brothers, and then there were the cousins. And the date — would she want a fall wedding? A New Year's Eve wedding? They can be so romantic. Of course they had to allow enough time for Pre-Cana.

No one had ever been this excited to do anything for Lucy. What would her mother's reaction have been? She tried to imagine Mrs. Donato, her mother-in-law-to-be, having this conversation at the kitchen table with Marge. Marge distrusted happy people; she assumed them dimwitted. Try as she may, Lucy couldn't even imagine Marge opening the front door for Mrs. Donato, let alone making her coffee. When Anne had called their mother to tell her she was engaged, Marge's only response was, "Remember to send your mother an invitation." Then, when the wedding invitation did arrive, informing them that the ceremony and reception were in New Jersey, "How the hell am I supposed to get there? Does she even want us there?"

While they waited for the valet parking, Tony's parents held hands like high school sweethearts hoping to sneak off. Lucy wondered if they'd been this affectionate throughout their marriage or if something — retirement, an almost-empty nest, the smell of the Atlantic's salt air, fear of death — made them frequently touch each other to make sure the other was still there within reaching distance. If her parents had had the opportunity to grow old together, would they have been like this? If, despite Marge's indifference, Joseph had continued to be affectionate, would something in her have softened? Would she have resigned herself to his love? Joseph did love Marge. Lucy was certain, although she couldn't say why he did. Anne's explanation came to mind. As usual, Lucy pushed the thought of her father being dishonest down deep into herself, somewhere below her ribcage, and ignored it.

She thought of Anne and Brad at Christmas, how they acted toward each other after eight years of marriage. Their motions were in reaction to one another's but polarized as they moved about their festively decorated home, providing for their guests, like magnets repelling from each other. Always on opposite sides of the room, always in motion at the same time. Connected but apart.

Brad had been everything the Pescitellis were not and because of that, it seemed, he was her sister's ideal. Sitting there at their dining room table, adorned with candles and a centerpiece of poinsettias and ivy, smelling of lemon furniture polish, Anne had the life of a respectable, educated, single-home-dwelling woman. But this woman had no longer looked at her husband lovingly, no longer looked him in the eye. She had been polite. He had been pleasant as always, and seemed eager to please Anne, to regain his former glory, but he had not succeeded that evening.

Tony's parents dropped them off at Lucy's house, saying they understood the young couple wanted a little alone time together on such a night, but that they'd see Tony for the eleven o'clock news. At nearly forty years old, Tony still played this game with his parents. Lucy thought it was sweet, appropriate, and she wanted them to think of her as the ideal daughter-in-law, as a virgin who cared for her sweet dying mother. Lucy received a final parting kiss from Mrs. Donato.

Once inside, they went quietly and directly to her bedroom, ignoring the sounds of Anne cooking her dinner in the kitchen. Tony began to undress.

"I didn't think I could have pulled it off without them being there. Was that okay?" he said. He was calmer now that his energy was focused on something with a known outcome.

"Yeah. They're family. Right?" Lucy said as she pulled her pants down and sat on the bed.

Tony was already under the covers, patting her side of the bed in invitation. It had been a long day, filled with excitement, and the sun hadn't even finished setting. She looked at Tony and smiled. Her future husband, the father of her children. From the nightstand — the same one that still held all the holy cards she collected over the years from funerals, the ones with the prettiest pictures, the sweetest prayers — she took a condom.

"We don't want to ruin your mother's wedding plans," she said. Tony laughed, took it from her, and pulled her on top of him. Lucy thought about revealing her pregnancy scare of that morning, how she thought they might already be connected for the rest of their lives, but Tony held her left hand and kissed the engagement ring.

"Thanks," he said.

"Sure," she said. They both laughed. Then they made love following the same routine established the first night together. This night it felt sweeter; they looked at each other more often, kissed a little slower, softer. It was a quiet encounter, and once finished they both drifted into slumber.

Lucy dreamt she was in the old house, Marge's house, in the dining room with the hospital bed in its center. The room didn't exactly resemble the real room as it was, but she knew that was where she was supposed to be. She looked down and her hands were forcing down a pillow, an upholstered sofa seat cushion, still enclosed in plastic covering. She yanked back her hands, then swatted at the pillow, fearful of what or whom she'd discover. There lay her future mother-in-law, Mrs. Donato — dead! This time, the image on her shirt was a heavenly scene that resembled a grade-school art project. The clouds were cotton balls, and pastel cherubs held harps constructed of elbow macaroni painted yellow. The smell of Elmer's glue and wilting roses pervaded the room. Lucy shook the old woman's shoulders. She even slapped her face, but there was no response.

Just then, she heard snoring. Where was it coming from? She looked around the room. No one was there. Just the very dead Mrs. Donato. Tracking the noise, she stared at the murder weapon, which had fallen halfway under the hospital bed. She bent and pulled it out. There was an image of Mrs. Donato's face created by her makeup. The colors were smeared, but Lucy saw blue eye shadow, the rouge, and the matte pink lipstick. She bent to get a closer look and realized that the snoring was emanating from the undefined nose and the blurred mouth. Lucy touched her cheek where Mrs. Donato had kissed her. The snoring was getting louder. Suddenly Marge stood in the kitchen doorway, smoking, and stated calmly, "You used the wrong pillow," and then walked into the kitchen, smoke lingering in the doorway. The snoring continued, and now Lucy heard music — the *Million Dollar Movie* theme.

Tony rolled over and tossed his arm across Lucy's chest. She sprang up. He was snoring. The television was on downstairs. After she caught her breath and calmed her heart, she woke up Tony. He was late for his parents; already she was ruining her standing with them. As he dressed, the dream came back to her and she felt guilty. In reality she liked his mother; why would she dream of killing her?

*   *   *

After Lucy locked the front door behind Tony, she sat next to her sister, who was lying in a tight ball on the couch. The bluish light of the television illuminated Anne's expressionless face. Her head rested on the bed pillow she brought downstairs to replace the plastic-covered sofa cushion. On the coffee table were a box of tissues, a glass of ginger ale, and Anne's dinner dishes. Lucy wanted to share her news with her sister or with Colleen, but really she wanted to share it with someone who would be excited for her, genuinely happy. Her sister was preoccupied with so much, the news of her father, the fire, and her pregnancy. Did she realize she was pregnant? If she knew, why would she keep it a secret? And why was she sad? Lucy thought that it might be unkind to be happy in front of her sister.

"So, how were they?" Anne mumbled, reaching for her drink.

"Really, really nice," Lucy said. "How are you feeling?"

"Okay," her sister said, her eyes focused on the TV. "I'm just tired."

Lucy kept her eyes on the screen too, and took a deep breath. She'd postpone telling her the news for the moment. "Does Brad know you're pregnant yet?"

There was a pause. "Not yet." Anne pulled her robe over her feet. "I'm going to wait until he gets back."

"Tell him in person. Of course," Lucy said. "Well, congratulations."

"Thanks. I was going to tell you."

"When are you due?"

"December, I guess." Anne returned the glass to the table. "I'll know for sure when I see the doctor."

Blue and green hues played on Anne's face. Lucy wondered if her sister was even interested in the program or just too lazy to get up and change the channel. Maybe she was just tired and not depressed. At least she didn't seem angry.

"I've got news too." Lucy held out her hand and wiggled her fingers as she had seen so many other women do. "Tony proposed."

Anne turned from the television and hugged Lucy. Lucy was surprised. It was a gentle, swaying hug, and Anne whispered into her ear. "I hope it turns out to be everything you want."

There were tears in her eyes when she pulled away. She wiped them quickly and glanced at Lucy. "Must be the hormones, huh?"

"Is everything okay, Anne?

"Yeah."

"You're going to keep the baby — aren't you?" Memories of Anne yelling about women's rights rang in Lucy's ears, Marge slamming the front door on her way out.

"Lucy, what kind of question is that? Yes. I just wanted to make sure everything was okay before I told anyone."

"Sorry." Lucy kept her other questions to herself. Did Brad know about the fire? Did Brad know Anne was here? Was Anne's marriage everything she'd hoped it would be?

They sat quietly. Lucy didn't know what to say next. This should be a happy moment. One sister engaged, the other expecting a baby. It was as if joy couldn't enter the house, as if Marge had sealed it tight with her ghostly presence.

"Can I get you anything before I head up?" Lucy said, standing.

"No thanks. I'm going up soon."

At the top of the steps, Lucy turned and went into the front bedroom, Marge's room, and sat on the bed. She turned on the lamp on her father's side of the bed and lit a cigarette. A marriage had taken place among these things. For Joseph, he'd spent twice as long as a bachelor than as Marge's husband. For her mother, her life was split in two — life before Joseph, life after him, or so Lucy had thought before. Now it seemed that it had been a stranger, Anne's father, who had created the defining split in Marge's life. Lucy's life had been split by Marge. Stubbing out her cigarette, Lucy stood. Tomorrow, she would truly start the other half of her life. Life without Marge, without Marge's things. Life with Tony.

Chapter Eighteen

The following morning when Jack knocked on her front door, without pause Lucy twisted her ring, hiding its diamond in her palm. She shoved her fist in her pants pocket. It was as if weeks ago, in that moment of close proximity at the bottom of the stairs, a lever had been forced down, setting in motion gears in her chest and stomach and maybe even, admittedly, the lower regions, starting a slow churning that was gaining momentum. As she awkwardly swung the screen door open with her right hand, she realized Jack was not alone — Mrs. Garrity, his aunt, stood smiling, holding a bakery box.

"I was told I'd be welcome if I came with sticky buns in hand," she said with raised eyebrows and a smile worthy of a denture commercial. "Raisins. No nuts?" In the sunlight, you could see through her red hair to her pale scalp. The white box glowed as she passed it to her nephew. Upon entering the house, she embraced Lucy, rocking her gently back and forth like a small child. After she released Lucy, she spun in a complete circle to take in the living room.

"My goodness, I half expect your mother, God rest her soul, to come in from the kitchen." She stopped her rotation and looked at Lucy, her head tilted to the side. A smile, the kind a mother gives to a child presenting refrigerator art, created ripples in her deflated cheeks. "I'm sure your mother would be very pleased to see that you thought fit to keep her things."

"Aunt Libby," Jack interrupted. "I told you Lucy's thinking of making some changes."

He skirted past his aunt and walked through to the kitchen. This was the first time Lucy had seen him wearing shorts this summer. While his legs were pale, they were muscular in an athletic way, not too bulky. She wondered if he ran or jogged or worked out, and quickly imagined him in each of those physical pursuits.

Mrs. Garrity walked toward the front window and bent in front of Marge's recliner, then squeezed its arms. For a moment, Lucy thought she was going to embrace the chair. Her fingers delicately ran across the amber ashtray nestled in its brass stand. Her eyes tear-filled, she whispered, "It doesn't have to be a dirty habit," and laughed softly.

With her hands grasped behind her back, she walked toward the wall of pictures, but not before briefly regarding her reflection in the large mirror that hung over the couch. "New change?"

"No. It came with the place."

Mrs. Garrity leaned forward as if viewing a collection at the art museum and studied the photographs she'd known well for years. Some people display books in their living rooms, or record albums or ceramic figurines. Marge had these half-dozen pictures and none of the other stuff — and so too, her daughter. Marge used to say that you could tell who your friends truly were because they would stop and look, and keep looking, even after they realized they weren't in any of the photographs and neither were their kids. And just as Anne had done on her first visit, Mrs. Garrity traced the bottom edge of Marge and Joseph's wedding picture frame, their black-and-white faces looking back at her.

"Who would have thought we were ever that young?" she said. "Ah, young love. You don't think then about who's going to die on who."

As she studied Lucy's and Anne's First Holy Communion pictures, she said, "It's amazing how much you take after your dad and how much Little Margie takes after your mother. Like the family's split down the middle. Where is your sister anyway? I'd heard she was staying with you."

"Anne. She goes by Anne now. She's sleeping," said Lucy.

"She's okay?" Mrs. Garrity said.

"Oh, she's fine."

Lucy led her old neighbor through the dining room — "Unbelievable, like walking into the past," — and into the mossy green kitchen where the similarity to the old house dropped considerably. Jack had put on a pot of coffee and placed the cinnamon buns on a plate at the center of the kitchen table. In the old kitchen there had been enough room to open both table leaves, making it a round, but in the new kitchen, the table resembled a one-winged bird. With three people, the room was crowded. The real estate agent, as Lucy recalled, labeled it "cozy."

Lucy wanted Colleen to be her Mrs. Garrity — someone to confide in, someone to provide a retreat from the world when necessary. But Lucy had to admit that it might never be that. For one thing, she still hadn't been inside Colleen's house. How would she tell Colleen about her engagement? Would Colleen be able to feign happiness for her?

Lucy, still handicapped with one hand in her pocket, went to the cabinet for coffee mugs.

"Uh-uh," Jack said. "I got everything. It's your birthday. We showed up uninvited. I insist you let me wait on you." He already smelt of coffee, sugar, and a slight warm odor of fresh perspiration.

Lucy sat at the table with her hands hidden on her lap. The ring made her finger itch, so she continued to twist it around and around. When she woke that morning, it looked strange to her. She'd never worn a ring before. In the shower, she'd scratched her scalp with it while washing her hair. With the appearance of Mrs. Garrity and Jack, she became aware that it signified a change in her life that other people, even strangers, would be privy to. She tried to think of a way of bringing up her engagement. She tried to think of why she hadn't already flung her hand in front of their eyes and wiggled her fingers as she'd done last night for Anne. Maybe she wanted it to be just between her and Tony right now. Enjoy the moment of having this secret. And, oh yeah, with Anne too. Or was it possible, even though so newly engaged, she was already experiencing the proverbial cold feet?

Jack gave them each a coffee mug and sat next to Lucy. She was book-ended by her two guests. Mrs. Garrity lifted her head to survey the kitchen now that her nephew no longer obstructed the view and spied Marge's recipe box on the windowsill.

"Oh my God, is that what I think it is?"

Lucy tracked her line of vision to the box. "Yes."

"May I?"

"Of course," Lucy said.

Mrs. Garrity pushed her chair out, making a screeching noise. Slowly she walked toward the box, fingers splayed, slightly crouched, as if approaching an exotic animal.

"Lucy, I brought some paint samples for you to look at for the living room," Jack said. "You said you'd be up for starting there first, right?"

"Uh-huh. Are you sure you want to do this?" Lucy said, wondering whether or not he'd want to do things for her if he knew she was engaged. Still, she couldn't decide if his kindness was just out of pity for a friend of the family.

"It'll be fun. My birthday gift to you. We can do it next weekend if you want. I'll bring some music. We could order Chinese take-out maybe? How's that sound?" He was digging through his backpack on the floor next to his chair.

135

His aunt had returned to the table and opened the recipe box slowly. Her mouth hung open slightly and then gradually curled into a smile as if she'd discovered a tiny smoking Marge inside. After running her finger back and forth over the tops of the index cards, she pulled one out, keeping its place with another finger. Clearly, she remembered who Marge was.

She read aloud:

Saturday
1. Bathroom cleaning (Saturdays, so that the tub is clean for Saturday night bath). Don't kid yourself. Get out the bleach and the bathroom tile toothbrush. It's the only way to clean the grout.

"Oh, my God. I can hear her voice saying that." Mrs. Garrity laughed, not continuing on with the extensive instructions. She caressed the card with her thumb and continued quietly, speaking into her chest, "And when your mother first showed up here, so young, she didn't know the first thing about keeping house. She said her mother never made her do anything; she had some big plans for Marge." She cleared her throat. "Do you use these, Lucy?"

"Sometimes. For the recipes," Lucy said. Most everything, recipes included, she knew by heart. The last time she referenced them was the morning of the stoop cleaning. After the Delvecchio sisters had questioned her cleaning method, Lucy checked to see if Marge insisted upon using bleach. As it turned out, she did. The stoop hadn't been scrubbed since that morning. If Lucy did add bleach to the bucket, her neighbors would surely take it as a victory.

"Oh, I didn't know there were recipes in here," Mrs. Garrity said as she replaced the card. She continued flipping through, as if turning the yellowing pages of a photo album or scrapbook and recalling vacations, graduations, and reunions.

"Now who did she write these for?" Jack said, wiping away sugar sticking to his chin. "She didn't need reminders and Lucy knew how to do all those things. Did Marge expect that some alien would be pulled from space and made to clean her house precisely as she did or else face imprisonment? Not that there would be much of a difference." He glanced at Lucy, and his smile drained from his face. "I mean, in that particular scenario."

Lucy bit into her bun, rubbing the sweetness against the top of her mouth. Had she in truth betrayed her own feelings for Jack by saying yes to Tony? The manner in which he could poke fun at her mother without cruelty was comforting to Lucy. Coming from someone else, it would have upset her. Coming from Anne, for example. But Jack knew Marge, and despite that liked her. He didn't assume that Marge had created the cards for the daughter she thought incompetent. Of course, Marge thought most everyone incompetent; it was just that she lived with Lucy. A raisin fell from the cinnamon-laced dough as Lucy went to take another bite. She instinctively grabbed it, with her left hand.

"What! What's this?" Mrs. Garrity grabbed Lucy's wrist. "Is it?"

"Yes," said Lucy, resisting the instinct to jerk her hand away.

"Oh, I had no idea you were dating. I mean seriously." She looked at her nephew, annoyed he'd forgotten to mention this delicious morsel to her. "No, I mean at all."

"It just happened last night," Lucy said.

"Aunt Libby," he said. He ran his fingers through his thick wavy hair. "Why wouldn't she be dating?"

For a moment, Lucy felt as though this was a discussion between the two of them. She squeezed behind Jack's chair to refill her mug and lit a cigarette. It was hard to create distance in the confines of the room. She couldn't see Jack's face. Didn't want to.

"And here we are barging in on your birthday when I'm sure you have plans with your fiancé," Mrs. Garrity said. She pulled her cigarette case from her purse (it was the same as Marge's only a dark brown, tobacco) in what seemed an act of camaraderie, or fabricated nonchalance. Smokers versus the nonsmoker.

"No. Actually he's spending the day with his parents. They're selling their house. The realtor's coming by today."

Jack grabbed another cinnamon bun from the center plate and took a large bite. Lucy watched his ears wiggle slightly as his jaw worked. Why hadn't she told him about Tony? Why had she concealed the ring? Was secrecy contagious? Hereditary?

"Well, that does sound like he's a nice son. How long have you known him? If you don't mind my asking? Is he from St. Peter's?"

"No. St. Catherine's. About two months."

"My." Mrs. Garrity repositioned the remaining bun on her plate and took another drag off her cigarette. "Of course, that's eons compared to your mother's courtship. Right?"

Lucy didn't say anything. Mrs. Garrity's cigarette was accumulating ashes so Lucy returned to the table and positioned the ashtray between their plates. She hadn't thought about her mother as having a courtship, particularly after Anne had told her the reason for her parents' marriage. Jack pushed back his chair and crossed his legs as he looked to his aunt.

"You do know the story of how your parents met?" Mrs. Garrity said.

"No," said Lucy.

"Oh, it's so romantic." Mrs. Garrity placed her cigarette in the ashtray and handed her empty mug to her nephew, who remained quiet. "Your mother was in Washington, D.C., the Capitol. On her way home, she boards the train and sits next to your father. They begin talking. They talk the whole way from D.C. to Philadelphia. They tell each other their dreams, their secrets. Things they never told anyone else."

Jack refilled their mugs, then sat and slowly stirred sugar into his coffee. Listening to Mrs. Garrity, Lucy stole glances of him, wondering if he was bored with the story or upset about her engagement. Suddenly, she wanted to be alone with him, to force him to look at her and tell her what he was thinking. Was he upset? Jealous? It was fantasy, she told herself. It was fear that conjured these emotions.

"Well, what can I say, there was chemistry. Your mother knew she'd found a real future and your father, well, it was love at first sight. When the train arrived at 30th Street Station, your father gave his hand to your mother to help her off the train and found himself proposing. They were married two weeks later. Such a beautiful story. I'm sure she told you. You must have forgotten."

"I guess," said Lucy. She imagined a young Marge being gently swayed on that train, staring out the window watching houses pass by, just as she herself had done on the bus to Center City. But on this journey Marge knew for certain she was pregnant, knew for certain that the father didn't want her or the baby. Then, Joseph, a stranger, asked to sit beside her. Did he ask because he recognized that she was alone and scared? Could two people fall in love in the course of a train ride from D.C. to Philadelphia? Did they love each other then or at the end? How do you know you love someone?

"Marge told me they met on a train," Jack said. "And that Joseph seemed like the kindest person she'd ever met, which, of course, she had a hard time trusting."

Anne appeared in the kitchen doorway. In her bare feet, she was inaudible. At times, Lucy felt she was living with a ghost. Two ghosts. Anne's green robe clashed with the moss kitchen tiles. The robe, Lucy realized, was kelly green, the color she had folded over and over again when she went through her mother's closet. The sisters exchanged glances. Lucy knew Anne had been listening and hoped that her scowl would silence her sister, but to no avail.

"Why was our father in D.C.?" Anne said.

"Oh, visiting an old army buddy from the war, I think," Mrs. Garrity said, as if Anne had been there the whole time.

Anne smiled, but didn't turn to Lucy. She jerked her head up slightly with raised eyebrows to Jack in what seemed half greeting, half invitation to spar.

Mrs. Garrity continued. "It always reminded me of that Claudette Colbert and Clark Gable movie, except they were on a bus I think . . . "

"And our mother. What business did she have down there?" Anne said.

"Well, to be honest, if you must know," Mrs. Garrity looked to Anne, whose eyes were cast downward, her head resting against the door frame, then to Lucy who offered a nervous smile. Certain she had an agreeable audience of at least one, she continued, "she went to see an old beau." She inserted a dramatic pause. "Sad really. He'd fallen in love with her, you see, over the summer before he left for college, a bright boy, head over heels, they say, and was threatening to drop out of school and ruin his life just to be with her. He couldn't bear being apart from her."

Anne laughed. Lucy took another drag of her cigarette.

Mrs. Garrity continued, her voice slightly raised. "She went down there to talk some sense into him, make him think about his future. He, of course, proposed. She refused. He begged, threatened suicide. But you know how practical your mother was. She knew what was best for him. God bless that woman, always so selfless. She didn't leave him until he promised not to do any harm to himself."

"No. I know she never told me that one," Anne said, shifting in the doorway. "But, you forget to mention that dear old practical, selfless Marge was already pregnant with me on that train."

Jack's mug clunked on the tabletop. Mrs. Garrity's head jerked as if a car had backfired, her face sunk in.

"Where did you get that?" she said through a clenched jaw.

"From dear old Marge herself," Anne said.

Mrs. Garrity tapped the tip of her cigarette into the ashtray, slowly extinguishing it. Lucy couldn't tell whether Mrs. Garrity was upset that Anne had ruined her romantic tale or if she was surprised by the news of the pregnancy. Did she know all of Marge's secrets? Had Marge lied to her? Did Mrs. Garrity feel that combination of confusion and anger and disbelief that Lucy and Anne had encountered in the past few months? Had Marge betrayed their friendship by confiding in another?

"They loved each other." Mrs. Garrity closed the recipe box and returned it to its proper place, as if it needed to be protected from Anne. She took a deep breath and rubbed her hands along the sides of her hips. "They took care of each other."

Maybe Mrs. Garrity had known all of Marge's secrets.

"She was," Anne hissed, "dumped. And she was forever bitter about it."

"I'd better be on my way," Mrs. Garrity said, spiking her cigarette case into her purse. "Happy birthday, Lucy, and congratulations. Come by sometime soon? We can talk about the wedding if you'd like."

"Sure, that sounds great," said Lucy.

Mrs. Garrity passed Anne in the doorway. "Margaret Anne."

Jack slid the paint samples in front of Lucy as they both stood.

"Are you sure you're still up for fixing up the place?" Lucy asked.

"Yeah," said Jack, distracted. They squeezed by the silent, unmoving Anne and walked to the front door. Mrs. Garrity was already outside.

"Congratulations, Lucy," he said, "He seems like a good guy." Jack descended the front steps.

After he'd taken a few steps, Lucy said, "Did you know, Jack? I mean about my mother?"

"We'll talk next Saturday," he said, shaking his head no, still walking, pointing to his aunt who'd already arrived at his car.

Once again a happy occasion destroyed, turned inside out.

When Lucy returned to the kitchen, Anne had usurped Mrs. Garrity's chair and sat eating one of the cinnamon buns. "These are good."

"What is your problem?" Lucy said. "You're going to have an angry baby if you keep this up."

"Where'd you get that?" Anne shook her head. "That woman would rather tell stories than tell the truth."

"So what? Let her have her stories." Lucy wondered if her sister woke up this angry or if it was Mrs. Garrity's story alone that had her so riled up.

"Lucy, you don't live in the real world."

Anne was one of those people who thought her life was more genuine, her emotions more intense and true, than anyone else's, merely because they were hers. She lacked the ability to empathize. No one had it as hard as she did. No one was more misunderstood by the ignorant masses. Human existence was a competition of whose life proved more tragic.

"You're so naïve. You have no idea what goes on in the big bad world out there." Anne stood and flung her arm toward the front of the house, toward the dining room.

"Life happens in small places too," Lucy said. "Life happens here."

Anne merely glanced at her sister; she had the same ability as their mother to end a conversation with a look.

Lucy grabbed her purse and left. Standing on the stoop, she felt exiled from her own house. She closed her eyes and swallowed hard. When she opened her eyes, she realized the Delvecchio sisters were both looking up at her from their lawn chair stations at the bottom of their stoops. There was no peace. No privacy.

"Ladies," Lucy said as she descended the steps and crossed the narrow street. She needed to escape the joylessness her sister had reintroduced to her life. For a moment, she felt uneasy, not remembering which house was Colleen's, like in grade school when she'd enter a classroom and stand in the back, not being able to recall her assigned seat, the one she'd sat in every-day for months. Then she caught sight of one of Tiffany's dolls in the bay window. Colleen's screen door was ajar, the storm door open. Lucy called in and then knocked on the bent aluminum door, which rattled against its frame. Her audience watched closely.

"What?!" called Colleen from inside.

"It's Lucy." She could hear the old ladies talking to each other, but she couldn't make out their grumbled words, something about noise.

Colleen opened the door, saying as she walked away, "I see Tweedledee and Tweedledum are out."

Inside, Lucy felt like she was entering Miss Havisham's mansion. Marge had been a big fan of *Great Expectations*, the movie. Lucy always remembered the cobweb-covered, mouse-infested wedding cake. Only in Colleen's house, there was no sign that hope, or the promise of love, had ever existed. The place was just a mess. Tiffany's practically life-size dollhouse, bright pink convertible, and plastic sliding board were strewn across the living room and dining room floors. Shoes were tossed under tables; T-shirts and pink princess costumes were stuck into the corners of the couch cushions. In the kitchen, their final destination, where Colleen sat at the table and clasped her coffee mug, dishes and take-out containers were stacked up in the sink, on the counter and the table.

"Are you okay?" Lucy asked.

"Now you know why I'm always at your house." Colleen chortled.

"Where's Tiffany?"

"With the asshole." Colleen was consistent with her ex-husband's nickname. "He takes her for a few weeks in the summer."

"Oh," Lucy said, wondering where it was that he lived. Despite his nickname, he seemed to be a good father. Perhaps he had trapped Colleen.

Lucy removed a pile of newspapers, crayon drawings, and mail off one of the kitchen chairs and sat down. In her house, Colleen helped herself to anything she wanted, but Lucy didn't feel comfortable helping herself in Colleen's kitchen. For one thing, she didn't know where anything was. For another, she wasn't certain there was a clean coffee mug or glass available. Colleen didn't offer her anything. Lucy wasn't sure where to begin so she pulled her cigarettes out and offered one to Colleen. This wasn't the reception she was hoping for. The clutter added to her confused mental state.

Lucy held out her lighter for Colleen to light her cigarette. Colleen scraped a stray bit of tobacco from her tongue. Her lips were pale and dry, her skin blotchy. There were dark purplish rings under her eyes and Lucy wondered if they were from lack of sleep or illness or drinking. Then she realized that this was the first time she'd seen her friend without makeup. Colleen looked rough, unfinished. Even when they'd run mundane errands together, Colleen wore a full face of makeup and had her hair teased or pulled into a taut ponytail.

Colleen dragged the large overflowing plastic ashtray over crumpled paper napkins and crusty utensils so that it sat between them. The head of a Ken doll lay in the middle of the pile of extinguished butts, his cheek and ear indented with a burn mark, covered in ashes.

"Did I tell you he's getting remarried?" Colleen pushed hair behind her ear.

"No. I'm sorry." Lucy said as she looked for the trashcan. Maybe it was in the cabinet under the sink. The doll's head was looking directly at her as if pleading for help, expecting that this was not the worst of his fate. Or perhaps warning her of her own fate.

"Fuck, Lucy!"

"What?"

"What the hell is that?" Colleen pointed to the engagement ring. "Don't tell me you're engaged? Don't tell me you're marrying the first guy you fucked?"

"Colleen!" Lucy said. "How can you talk like that?"

"Oh come on. What? Did you expect me to squeal?" She took a drag of the cigarette and twisted her mouth so that smoke shot out away from Lucy. "Jump up and down? Men suck. All men suck. Even your Jack."

"Tony," Lucy corrected.

"Whatever. Jack thinks he was immaculately conceived like Jesus or something."

"You mean like the Blessed Mother."

"Huh?"

"Immaculate Conception. Conceived without original sin. That's Mary."

"Jesus had original sin?"

"No. He's God."

"Are we really talking religion?" Colleen said.

"Are we really talking about Jack? I'm marrying Tony." For a moment, Lucy considered that Colleen might have feelings for Jack.

"Makes no difference to me who you marry. I'll show up if you want." Colleen snorted her nasal laugh, "Even be a bridesmaid. I'm always up for a party. But don't think I'm going to act like this is the best thing that ever happened to you."

"What if it is? What if this is what makes me happy?" Lucy started collecting the used napkins into a pile.

"Then, I guess," Colleen exhaled smoke onto the end of her cigarette and watched the embers light up, "you're an idiot."

"This isn't even about me. It's about the asshole."

"Who?"

"Your ex-husband getting married," Lucy said, although her mind was still mulling over Colleen's possible crush on Jack.

"Oh, Bob. No. He was an asshole before he told me he was getting married."

"Besides, you don't seem to be so happy and you're single."

"At least I don't have to cook and clean for some slob and then pretend to find him sexy at the end of the day after washing his shitty underwear."

Lucy looked around the kitchen and started laughing. "Yeah, you got that right."

Colleen laughed.

"You don't need a man to make you complete or to fulfill you or whatever, you know."

"I'm the one who's been living without men, remember?" Lucy stood and confirmed that the trashcan was under the sink.

"What's the rush, is all?" Colleen remained seated.

"He asked." Lucy ran water over the dishes in the sink and rinsed out the take-out containers. Cleaning calmed her.

"You don't have to do that."

"It's okay. I'm good at it."

"No really. I don't see the point of housekeeping when I'm alone."

"Colleen, I don't get it. I mean you fixed me up, put me in a dress, and sent me out into the world. Didn't you want me to meet somebody? Wasn't that the point?"

"I don't know. I thought we'd have fun, not get married." She put out her cigarette without further injury to Ken's head. "Let me do that." Colleen didn't budge.

"It's all right. I don't want to go home anyway."

Chapter Nineteen

Marge's purse hung on the headboard of her bed, its contents the same as when she used it everyday, minus a pack of cigarettes. The bedroom was undisturbed since Jack finished the plasterwork. Each week Lucy put on fresh sheets, folding them into meticulous hospital corners. Each week, she dusted and vacuumed. Only the closet and drawers were altered, emptied. Still, as she pulled the camel-colored address book from its compartment, Lucy felt like a child sneaking about, stealing change for the ice cream truck.

It was quiet when Lucy arrived at work. Mrs. Layne's body was in the small parlor awaiting her wake and funeral the following morning. Before heading out, Ralph told Lucy that Mr. Botti had someone in his office. The old gray IBM typewriter buzzed and hummed when she turned it on, its round head whirling until it rested at the far left. There was only a slim stack of invoices to be typed. After a few moments with Ralph clearly gone and no sound from Mr. Botti's office, Lucy took out the address book and searched Marge's precise printing for the same number she'd looked for the last time she'd turned these bumpy pages.

The answering machine picked up and Anne's recorded voice announced, "You've reach the Andersons. We are not available right now. Please leave a message." Her sister's voice was carefree and energetic, void of the anger and exhaustion of the past few weeks. It made Lucy curious as to when it had been recorded — a month ago, a year ago, longer? She hung up. It hadn't occurred to her what she would say if she got the answering machine or if she got Brad on the line.

Anne's story about the fire was bogus; Lucy knew this. And knowing this made the possibility that Brad was in the country, not away on business, greater. As Tony noticed that first night, her sister's luggage didn't smell of smoke. There were no news reports about a fire in Anne's development. Not once had Lucy found her sister on the phone with the fire department or the insurance company or contractors. Anne was lying. But why? When she first arrived, Lucy could understand Anne making up a lie, being overwhelmed by the news Marge had mailed to her. With Tony, a stranger there, maybe Anne didn't want to talk about family business. Who was he to her? But now, Anne knew Tony was going to be her brother-in-law, and Lucy knew that her father was not Anne's father, and Lucy knew that Anne was pregnant. Now, couldn't Anne admit that there wasn't a fire? It wasn't as though Anne constantly brought up the fire. And since Lucy knew about her pregnancy, Anne had stopped using smoke inhalation as an excuse for her fatigue and her need for assistance.

She considered calling Brad's office to ask if he was away on business, but her mother's address book listed only Anne and Brad's home number. If only she could remember the name of his company. Despite her efforts to pay attention to his talk of work, her mind had wandered each time. He just used so many words each time he opened his mouth. She was almost certain it was located in King of Prussia. Some type of financial thing. Even if she remembered what kind of work he did, she didn't think it would be listed in the yellow pages. Jack would remember. She wanted to call him — about so many things.

When the phone rang, Lucy shoved the address book into her bag.

"Anthony Botti's Funeral Home. May I help you?" she said.

"Good evening. May I ask who it is I'm calling again?" The voice sounded like an anchorman's.

"This is Anthony Botti's Funeral Home."

"Anthony Botti's?" There was a pause. To Lucy, this was nothing unusual. This was a place no one was ever really prepared to call. "Oh," he said. "Lucy? Lucy Pescitelli? Is that you?"

"Yes?" She looked around her as if the caller was in the room. Mr. Botti's door was still closed. Mrs. Layne lay still in the small parlor.

"It's your brother-in-law. Brad Anderson. I just got in and I saw this number on the machine and I thought . . . well I thought, maybe it was Anne calling. Have you heard from Anne?"

"I, well, I . . . " Lucy suddenly felt that she'd betrayed her sister.

"Have you seen her?" he asked. "She wouldn't tell me where she was going."

Mr. Botti's door opened.

Glenn Lepper dwarfed the doorframe. His bus driver uniform looked wrinkled and flaccid, clinging to his slumped shoulders. Lucy hadn't seen him since he and his mother came back to the house after Marge's funeral. She hadn't thought of him since her bus trip to Center City.

"I'm at work, Brad. I have to go."

"Lucy, just tell me if she's okay. Is she with you?"

"There's someone here. I have to go." Lucy hung up the phone and hoped Brad would not call back. The sound of the phone hitting the cradle brought Glenn's eyes to Lucy. He smiled faintly at her as he shook Mr. Botti's hand.

"Lucy," Glenn said, walking toward her, leaning slightly to his left as though his mother was on his arm whispering in his ear. Lucy stood and he embraced her, surprising her. He was the biggest person to have hugged her in her life, over a foot and a half taller than she was, over a hundred pounds heavier. She surprised herself in returning the embrace without reserve. He felt as she might have guessed, had she ever predicted this moment, like braided bread — warm, soft, yet firm, as if you could unravel him in buttery layers.

"I'm so glad you're here," he said, letting go and practically collapsing in the armless chair next to her desk. "You may be the only person who'd understand."

Lucy wasn't sure what to say. "Your mother, Glenn?"

He nodded. "I found her in the kitchen. I thought she'd nodded off writing her letters. You know she still kept in touch with friends from her school days in the old country."

"I didn't know. That's sweet."

Glenn paused, kneading his knees. "You don't expect them to die, do you? Really? I mean, logically, we're all going to die. We know our parents die, even our mothers. But it seemed my whole life was settled. This was my life." He looked up at the ceiling in an attempt to drain his tears back into his head. They ran down his cheeks. "I really loved her, you know. I can say that to you, can't I? I really loved her."

"Of course you did. She was a lovely woman." Lucy wasn't sure whose words were being transmitted through her, but they seemed to be the ones he needed to hear.

"I mean, some people think it's odd, you know, to live with your mother. But we got along good. And after Dad died, it just didn't make sense for me to leave. We needed each other. We liked each other."

"You were lucky to have each other."

"It was that way for you too, wasn't it?"

"Yes," Lucy said. She'd never asked herself why she'd stayed. The topic, she realized, scared her.

"What do I do now? I don't know where to begin." He rubbed his face, moving the flesh into half-moons with his hands.

"It'll be okay." She handed him a tissue and patted the emblem on his upper arm.

"You moved. Why did you move?"

"We thought it was best." There. A lie, but a brief one. Changing the subject seemed the right thing to do. "I've managed since then. A new house, a few new friends. I'm engaged now."

He blinked at her. She couldn't tell if she'd said the wrong thing. She had thought that he would want to hear that it all works out in the end. There can be happiness, even for an orphan. Maybe it was too soon. He wanted her to still be mourning, to be lost in despair without her mother.

"Your mother loved you very much," she said, holding out her hand for the used tissue. She tossed it in the trashcan and gave him a new one.

"She was a great woman. It's strange when they become dependent on you, isn't it?" Glenn said. "I mean, you're the child and they're the parent, and then suddenly you wake up one morning and everything's switched. You're in charge. You decide what needs to be fixed and you make the doctors' appointments. And you worry that you're doing the right thing. Mama was pretty healthy, considering her age. I don't know how you did it with your mother."

"My mother was pretty healthy . . . despite the cancer." Lucy recognized how stupid that sounded before she finished the sentence, but Marge had been in control until the very end.

Glenn stood and hesitated, looking at the front door. His mother most probably had already been settled in the basement of the funeral home. Possibly for the first time in his life, he would be going home to an empty house. When Lucy rose from her chair, he immediately embraced her, as if seeking physical support, as if she could carry him.

"Can I call you? Just to talk," he said, passing her the tissue.

"Of course." Lucy walked him to the door.

*　　*　　*

Water from the spray bottle created a mini-sun shower on the floral wreaths as Lucy went over her conversation with Glenn, word for word. That she had comforted him in some small way was unexpected. With others, she was usually quiet, merely nodding and offering a sympathetic smile. This evening with Glenn, she said the right things and, more importantly, she left out the wrong things. At least, she hoped she had. Would he call her? And what would they talk about? Dead mothers? She imagined Glenn coming home from work and sitting across the dinner table from his mother, telling her stories about his passengers that day. His mother nodding and smiling, proud of the man her son had become. Lucy loved her mother. But did they like each other? Enjoy each other's company? Did she stay just because it was easy? Did she stay so Marge could take care of her?

The phone rang and Lucy saw she'd created a puddle in front of a round wreath from Mrs. Layne's friends at the senior center. Water cascaded off the ribbon. It wasn't Brad, just someone calling to ask if the funeral home would be air-conditioned for tomorrow's service. She dabbed up the water spot on the rug with paper towel, then vacuumed around Mrs. Layne's coffin. She imagined Brad at her house now, pounding on her front door, calling out Anne's name. The Delvecchios and Colleen hanging out their windows watching the show. Anne would never forgive her. She lined up the white folding chairs in straight rows and decided to leave a little early. It wasn't until after she turned on the answering machine and shut off the lights that she realized that Brad didn't know where she lived now. Anne had been gone for weeks and he hadn't chased her down, so it was unlikely that he'd be doing some watered-down suburban version of Stan Kowalski on her front stoop.

But outside, Lucy discovered Brad standing under the awning where Tony had stood the night of their first date. At least he wasn't at her house.

"Could I buy you a coffee? Could we talk?" he said, as he opened a large golf umbrella and took her elbow.

The rain sounded loud on his oversized umbrella. As she led him toward the coffee shop that she and Tony had gone to that first night, their shoes slapped against the sidewalk, spitting water. Brad was unusually quiet, which made her uneasy.

"Do you remember Glenn Lepper from the old neighborhood? He was the big guy at my mother's funeral," Lucy said.

"The name sounds familiar," Brad said, watching his feet.

"He came in the funeral home tonight. His mother died. We talked for a while. He asked if he could call me. To talk about our mothers, I guess. We're both orphans, now." As Lucy stated this fact, it occurred to her that Anne was not. Anne had a living parent. Did Brad know?

"He's interested in you."

"I don't think so. I told him I was engaged." Lucy watched Brad's face. No reaction. He must have assumed that she made it up so as not to be bothered.

"Men take advantage of those situations, " he said after a moment.

"Not Glenn," she said. "Besides, it was his situation, not mine."

"He had your sympathy."

"I think he just felt alone."

"Exactly."

Lucy stopped in front of the shop. Brad opened the door for her and collapsed the umbrella. They took the table by the window. He was obviously distracted. He'd come to talk about Anne, not Lucy. Still, Lucy was disturbed by his remarks. The idea that everyone had a motive for his or her actions all the time disturbed her. The idea that she was oblivious to them and had to have Brad point out what he saw as obvious disturbed her. The idea that she lacked motives in a world where, apparently, everyone else was looking out for himself or herself, disturbed her. But hadn't she had some motive behind calling Brad? Didn't she want Anne and her perpetual misery out of the house?

She ordered cappuccinos and biscotti as Tony had done. Brad was flushed, which made his white-blond eyebrows and lashes stand out more. When the food arrived, Lucy blew on her hot beverage while Brad stared out the window as if watching home movies, his expressions conveying nostalgia and hurt. Lucy found herself searching for something in the darkness beyond the spotlights thrown by the streetlamps. Marge had said that she didn't trust Brad. He was rich and over-educated by Marge's standards anyway, and, therefore, weak. Brad, Marge had predicted, would disappoint Anne at some point. In part, because Anne placed too much hope in him. Of course now Lucy understood that Marge wasn't prophesying, but merely recounting her own disappointment.

"So how's work?" Lucy said.

"I love Anne."

"Okay."

"What I did. What I almost did. Is unforgivable. Inexcusable. I'm fully aware of that. Nonetheless, I want the opportunity to explain. Not that I even deserve that much, I realize. But I would like that opportunity to tell her that it had never happened before. That it hadn't happened then. I don't know whether she'd believe me or not. If I had come upon such a scenario with her and another man, I'd conclude the worst. I would. Wouldn't anybody?" He paused, although he wasn't seeking a response. He picked up his cappuccino and then placed it back in its saucer. "I don't know why I told you that."

Lucy was silent; she still didn't know what to say. Marge had been right. Words weren't coming to her as they had earlier at the funeral parlor. But then, Glenn hadn't said anything surprising, anything she didn't already know. Brad had cheated on her sister, or almost cheated. That's why Anne was hiding out at her house.

"Anne's incredible. She's funny and kind, so kind, and smart and yet she retains an innocence. A belief in the basic goodness in people. I don't know anyone else like her. I would never set out to betray her. To hurt her. To destroy our marriage. Our lives."

She dunked a biscotti into the creamy surface of her cappuccino. Anne was funny? Innocent? This version of Anne had never revealed itself in the Pescitelli household. Lucy felt gypped.

"I remember seeing her when she first showed up at school," he continued. "A nice Irish-Catholic girl. I used to tease her that there was no way she was half Italian. It was as if she'd never wandered off that tiny street in South Philadelphia. I had the urge to protect her. I had the urge to give her the world. I took advantage, I'm certain. In some respects it was easy to impress her and in other ways I was constantly aware that I wasn't good enough for her. This was a person with beliefs, standards."

Listening to Brad's description of her sister, her half sister, she couldn't tell if Brad knew about Anne's true paternity. But ever since Lucy had learned that Anne was her half sister not her full sister, she had contemplated the term. She wondered if Anne had hidden part of herself, half of herself, the good half, the pleasant half, the funny half, the half that believed in the basic goodness in people.

He assumed that Lucy was privy to what had happened, or he didn't care if she wasn't. "I'm sure you hate me too. You are her sister."

"I don't hate you."

"Do you know where she is? I just never thought of her contacting you. I realize you are her sister, of course. But she's just never turned to family for help in all the time I've known her. I thought of friends, old co-workers. I even called a few resorts, but I've been checking the credit-card statements. She's spent no money. And I knew that she was all right. She's been sending me these postcards. So full of anger. But I knew she was all right." He shook his head and slowly turned his cup in its saucer.

Anne had actually left the house. More than once. To mail postcards. Lucy imagined her sneaking to the corner box in her robe.

"She's at your house? Isn't she?"

Lucy stirred the softening biscotti.

"Don't worry. I won't go there. I don't even know where it is," he said. "I do love her, Lucy."

"I know. I'll tell her."

"Maybe it was the pressure of trying to get pregnant for the past year, and Anne not working. The thought of infertility. The embarrassment of my own possible incompetence. Being at that point in my life, considering fatherhood and all its implications and panicking. It's not a reason. It's a terrible excuse. We would have had a child, given enough time. I'm still struggling with what could have brought me to that. I didn't plan it. But I didn't take control. I didn't stop it. Anne had to do that."

"Do you still want a baby?" Lucy said, studying his face.

"I want Anne," he said, finally looking at his sister-in-law.

*　　*　　*

When Lucy came into the house, Anne lay on the sofa watching a medical drama. The images on the screen were pale and fuzzy, since her sister never bothered to work with the antenna. In Marge's recliner, Lucy sat down and thought of what to say. Tony's duffle bag of laundry waited at the bottom of the stairs. He must have gone up to bed early in lieu of spending time with her sister. At the first commercial break, Lucy stood and lowered the volume, keeping her back to Anne.

"I saw Brad tonight." She flinched as she heard Anne shift on the plastic couch coverings. "That's why I'm late."

"Is he here?" Anne whispered.

"No."

"What did you tell him?"

"I didn't tell him anything. He did all the talking."

"So, he told you about the catering whore?"

"I guess." Lucy returned to the recliner.

"You didn't tell him I'm pregnant?"

"No."

Anne got up and turned up the volume. A premature baby had just been delivered and was being rushed to the NICU. The mother had been in a car accident. The father didn't know which one to stay with, which one would survive. There were a lot of sick or dead babies on the show this season.

Anne covered her eyes with her fists. "I don't know why I watch this."

"Are you going to tell him?" Lucy said. "He's the father. You should."

"I don't know."

"You have to talk to him. You're having his baby." Sitting in Marge's chair seemed to give her confidence. "And you can't stay here forever."

Anne took her hands away from her face. "I don't know what I'm going to do," she said into her lap.

"You need to decide something, sometime."

The medical drama ended and Lucy turned the knob to channel 6, the station she continued to watch religiously even after Marge's death. Her mother had truly instilled rituals in her. The sisters were silent as the eleven o'clock news blasted its theme song. Lucy wondered if Tony was awake, if he could hear them from the back bedroom. This man was to be her husband, yet she hadn't told him about Anne's pregnancy. She hadn't told him that her father wasn't Anne's father. After she spun the rabbit ears, the picture became clearer, although it was only in primary colors.

"How did he look?" Anne asked.

"A mess. Just a mess," Lucy said. "He said he loves you and that he still wants to have a baby with you."

The second story of the night, following a three-alarm fire at an apartment building, was about the Werewolf Boy.

"Mom followed this story. That poor little boy," said Lucy.

Anne looked at Lucy, "What do you mean?"

"She watched it when it was on the news, even read about it in the paper. On the night she died." Lucy paused. She had put that night out of her thoughts for so long. To say that Marge died felt like a lie. "She stayed up to see what he looked like after surgery, but they didn't have any pictures."

The news switched from a graphic to footage taken at the hospital. Anne pointed at the television screen. "Look."

"I am," Lucy said. Did her sister think there was a connection between Marge's interest in this South American boy and Lucy's hirsuteness too?

"No. Look at the doctor."

"What about him?"

"That's my father."

"What?" Lucy said.

With one hand on the boy's skull and the other under his chin, Dr. Eugene McCormick explained the next surgery the boy was to undergo. He was attractive and about their mother's age. There was a resemblance to Marge in his coloring and the shape of his face. Lucy had heard of people growing to look like their spouses after years of marriage. Was it possible that Marge and this doctor grew to resemble each other even though they'd been separated for over thirty years?

"She was watching him. Not the boy," Lucy said.

"You said Mom watched him the night she died?" Anne said. "That's eerie."

At that moment, Lucy wanted to tell her sister the truth, that Marge planned her death. Marge watched him that night. He was one of the last people she saw. Had Marge known that he would be on television? Was it a coincidence?

"Do you think it was her seeing him that made her die that night?" Anne asked, then quickly added, "I know that sounds ridiculous."

"No, it doesn't," Lucy said. "But she'd seen him before, at least once, I think, when the boy first arrived at the hospital." Lucy struggled to remember. Like everything else, she didn't know where to put the emphasis on Marge's things or actions. What clothes that Lucy had given away had been important to Marge? She surveyed the room; everything was as it was in the old house. What did any of it mean? What moments in time, in all those years living alone together, were significant? Had Marge seen him on television before?

"Do you think he could really be my father?" Anne asked.

Lucy caught a last glimpse of him before the commercial break. "You two do look alike. Besides, why would Mom make up such a thing?"

"Do you think that's why Mom didn't want me to go to college, or move away, or do or be anything?"

"What do you mean? As a way of punishing him?"

"I guess. But what would he know?" Anne mumbled as she swung her feet off the couch. "She said he wouldn't admit I was his."

A furniture store announced its upcoming Independence Day sale, and the sisters sat quietly.

"Too much is happening in my life," Anne said. "Do you know what I mean? It's like nothing significant happens for years and then, boom, everything happens."

"I know exactly what you mean."

Her sister continued as though uninterrupted. "I lose my mother, then she takes away the only father I've ever known, then my husband nearly cheats on me, and then after two years of unsuccessfully trying to get pregnant, I'm crashing at my sister's house, pregnant and alone. It's craziness. It's too much. I keep thinking I'm going to wake up and everything will be back to the way it was. But then, I wouldn't have the baby and I want the baby."

"And you want the baby to have a father? A father she knows?"

"I was so angry with him. When I needed him most, with all this going on, he messed up big time."

"It didn't happen. It may not have happened even if you hadn't shown up. And you're never going to figure it out sitting on my couch."

"I know." Anne stood. "I'm going to bed. I can't think anymore today."

Lit in the cool colors of the television light, her sister climbed the stairs into the darkness of the second-floor hallway. Lucy stayed in Marge's recliner and lit a cigarette, wondering if her mother was still somehow present, controlling things. Had Marge made the Werewolf Boy appear on the news this night? And if she had, what did it mean? Did she want Anne to stay with Brad or leave him? Meet her father or not? Was she secretly proud of Anne, and did she want Dr. Eugene McCormick to see how well Marge had done without him? How well their daughter had turned out? Lucy pushed back on the chair and raised her feet. Tonight maybe she'd fall asleep to the sounds of the *Million Dollar Movie*.

Chapter Twenty

More than a dozen paint samples were fanned across the kitchen table in strips of beige, white, pink, blue, green, orange, and brown, each with four gradations of the same color. Jack had already arrived, breakfast in hand, and Lucy still had not decided. Tony, when asked his opinion, was not interested in painting the living room, reiterating that he thought the house was fine as it was. But he understood women got into that stuff. "Go crazy," he instructed her.

"I brought a half-dozen. Is anyone else joining us?" Jack plopped down the brown paper bag next to Lucy's color wheel and pulled out two bagels.

"No. Just us. I thought I heard Anne earlier, but she hasn't come down, and I'm pretty sure she's not up for painting."

He placed a bagel in front of Lucy. "I hope you like everything-bagels."

"I don't know, never had one."

"I should have brought the standard, huh?"

"No. This is good. Something new."

"Really? I got cream cheese with scallions in it. That okay?"

"Great. Thanks."

"Still haven't decided?"

"No. Sorry."

"That's okay. We have plenty of prep work to keep us busy today. That mirror's going to take some time." He took a bread knife from the drawer and sliced the bagels in half. "Toasted?"

"Whatever you're doing," she said, fingering the color strips.

"Why don't you take out the ones you definitely don't want?" he said, pointing to the colors. "Process of elimination."

Lucy took out the green palettes, then the beiges, and finally the browns. That still left her with a half-dozen. She spread cream cheese on her bagel halves and took a bite. It was warm, chewy. She licked the cream cheese from her lips. Jack looked at her expectantly.

"It's good," she said. From the fan, she pulled a strip with warm golds and held it next to a bagel at the mouth of the paper bag. One of the squares matched the golden dough. "What do you think?"

"Hm-m," Jack said. He pulled another strip from the fan, whites, and held it next to the tub of cream cheese. "And for the trim?"

"I like it."

"To a delicious room," he said, raising his coffee mug. They clinked mugs and sipped.

The taste of onions and garlic and sesame and coffee permeated her mouth. She was really enjoying this morning. A sadness came over her as she thought that these moments would probably end after her wedding. Tony didn't appreciate her friendship with Jack; he might think it was inappropriate for his wife to have a male friend. Maybe that's why she hadn't mentioned Jack's participation in the day's home improvements. The more time Lucy spent with Jack, the more legitimate Tony's disapproval seemed.

"Congratulations," Jack said, settling into his chair with bagel and coffee. "I really didn't get a chance to say that the other day. So much was going on. But it's great news. I'm glad you're happy." He raised his mug again. While they had spoken briefly on the phone about the logistics of the day, they hadn't discussed the other morning's drama.

"Thanks," said Lucy, as she ran her fingers across the discarded color palettes. They were Marge's colors — the green of her clothing, the camel of her purse, the brown of her cigarettes.

"I should have brought champagne," Jack said. "We could have had mimosas."

"You don't think I'm rushing things?" she asked, and immediately regretted it.

"No, of course not." He licked cream cheese from the side of his bagel. "But, what a year you've had."

"I know."

"It's been amazing watching you. For all those years after your father died and Anne left, you were in Marge's shadow and now, finally, the light's directly on you. And you're radiant. And you're flourishing." He stopped, seemingly embarrassed. "Anyway, what do I know about relationships? I'm practically forty and not married. There's something to be said for not waiting."

Lucy didn't know what to say, but she was pleased with what he had said about her.

He reached around and pulled the coffee pot off the counter. "You'd be better off asking your sister a question like that."

A spontaneous laugh erupted from Lucy's throat.

"What did I say?" Jack said.

"Nothing. Anne and Brad have their problems, is all."

"Nothing serious, I hope."

"I think they'll be okay," Lucy said.

Jack played with the rejected color samples, matching different colors together, perhaps considering colors for his office. Right now, Lucy was the happiest she'd ever been in her life, despite all the deceit in her family. Tony loved her, openly, and no one had done that since her father. It felt good to be loved. But did she love him? And did that matter? In the end it seemed that it came down to taking care of each other, and she knew how to take care of Tony.

Still, sitting with Jack in the sunlit kitchen and eating breakfast was wonderful. Sadly, she felt her time with him was evaporating. With Tony, she knew that he wanted her, needed her. Jack never asked anything of her, never said if he wanted or needed her. To him, she was just a friend of the family, in need.

*   *   *

With mugs in hand, Jack and Lucy surveyed the living room and developed a plan of attack. The plastic furniture coverings, they agreed, would be left on as drop cloths and then discarded after the painting was done, which made Lucy wonder exactly what the furniture felt like. The smaller furniture without its own protective covering would be moved into the dining room. The wall-to-wall carpeting would serve the same purpose as the slip covers if the wood floor under it was in good shape.

"You knew about Anne's dad?" Lucy asked, as she collected doilies.

"I didn't. I did think it was weird when your mother asked me to wait for six months after the funeral, then mail that letter to Anne, " he said as he carried the ashtray stand into the dining room. "But it wasn't that shocking when I heard it come out of Anne's mouth. It kind of explains some things. Don't you think?"

"Uh-huh. We saw him, her dad, on the news the other night."

"Why was he on TV?" Jack stopped in the middle of the room.

"No, no. They weren't cuffing him and hauling him away," Lucy laughed.

"Good."

"Have you heard about the Werewolf Boy?" Lucy lifted the pope's picture from the wall.

Jack wrapped his arms around the back of the recliner and lifted with his legs. "Sure. It's unfortunate they call him that. Poor kid," he breathed out.

"The plastic surgeon's Anne's father."

"Really?" He walked past her.

"They do look alike." Carefully, Lucy separated the pictures with her fingers. Anne's Communion picture went on top of hers.

"So is Anne going to contact him?" The chair hit the floor with a thump. Another thump echoed upstairs. Both of them looked up.

"Do you think she fell out of bed?" Jack said.

"I don't think so." Lucy laughed again. "Maybe she's packing?"

"Huh." Jack rested his hands on his thighs and stretched his back.

"I don't know why my mother even told Anne," Lucy said. "My father loved her. He was a good father to her."

As she placed her parents' wedding picture on top of the others, she smiled at her father's face. It occurred to her that Marge had never hung Anne's wedding picture. She was certain Anne had given her mother a framed one for Christmas that year.

"I think it's good Marge told her," Jack said. "Obviously, it wasn't something she could talk about, even after all those years. But like I said, it explains some things."

At that moment Lucy wanted to tell Jack everything. All the secrets she'd been carrying, not just her own. Marge's suicide/murder, Anne's pregnancy, Brad's near-infidelity, the stories about Colleen, the rumors about Tony — she wanted him to hear it all, because Jack believed in forgiveness. Jack believed in redemption. For hadn't he known her all along? Hadn't he forgotten her past?

They worked in silence. Lucy placed the pictures facing up on the dining room table. Marge lay on her back, staring at the ceiling in a dining room again, this time with Joseph by her side. Jack pulled the heavy furniture to the middle of the living room. When Lucy removed the drapes from the front window, the sunlight showed particles of dust floating in the air. The curtains were heavy in her arms. She arranged them over the old stereo cabinet and glass-top coffee table that Jack had moved next to the sofa. Jack commented: "Now you're getting into it."

It felt good to dismantle the room.

Once the room was cleared and the large pieces covered, Jack tugged at a corner of the carpet.

"What do you think? Looks good," he said once he'd revealed a square foot of wood floor that was in decent shape.

"Let's do it." Lucy liked the idea of bare walls and bare floors, of being surrounded by the warm glow of bagels. However, that was as far as her imagination let her go. Try as she might, she could not place a single piece of furniture, old or new, in the room.

Jack brought the stepstool from the basement and placed it in front of the mirror.

"I hope this isn't as heavy as it looks," he said. "Can you come over and lean against it while I unscrew the top?"

Lucy stood between the step ladder and the mirror. The heat from her hands created ghostly forms against the gold flecks in the glass. Her face so close to the mirror made her uncomfortable; she closed her eyes. Jack was whistling. She could feel the warmth from his body.

"Can you take these?" he said as he stepped down from the ladder.

She turned, keeping her back against the mirror, and cupped her hand. He poured three screws into it. Jack and Lucy were standing face to face. As he bent to move the ladder, she cupped his face with her free hand and kissed him. He returned the kiss, placing his hands on her hips, stealing the oxygen from her blood, lighting every nerve ending. Jack pulled away.

"I'm sorry," he said, his mouth remaining in kissing distance.

"No. I'm sorry," Lucy said. They stood looking at each other, his hands still on her hips. She thought he might kiss her again. She might kiss him again. Instead, he turned, saying he needed something in the basement and would be right back. Lucy remained leaning against the mirror, not sure if it would come crashing down if she moved. She could still feel the kiss. It was different than with Tony. With Tony she was always aware that it was, indeed, his tongue in her mouth, the same tongue he used to dislodge a piece of stringy beef from his molars. With Jack it was all breath and heat. She thought she heard Anne upstairs. Her hands shook. She longed for a cigarette.

"Maybe I should go," Jack said upon his return. Lucy assumed he'd left to get a tool, but he came back empty-handed, with not even another screwdriver as an excuse.

"Please don't. I'm sorry," Lucy said, stepping away from the mirror. It creaked slightly, one corner separating from the wall. Both Lucy and Jack pressed themselves against the mirror.

"We'd better get this down first," he said.

Lucy held the mirror in place, her back toward him, as he quickly unscrewed the remaining screws. They pried the corners away from the wall. Cobwebs, much like the patterns embedded into the mirror's design, clung to its back and the wall. They stretched as Jack and Lucy lowered the mirror to the floor.

Lucy opened the front doors, and Jack took the end of the mirror closest to the door so that he would bear the weight down the front steps.

"Go ahead in, Mom," Tony's voice called out just as Jack nearly bumped into Mrs. Donato coming up the stairs.

"Oh, sorry," she said. "I must have the wrong house."

"No," Lucy managed to say under the weight of the mirror. "Excuse us for a sec."

"Oh, sure." Mrs. Donato moved to the sidewalk. "I brought bridal magazines for us to look through and start getting ideas. I've marked a few things." A stack of more than a dozen thick glossy magazines were cradled in her arms. There were so many ripped pieces of paper used as bookmarks sticking out, it looked like she was carrying a dried-out mop top.

Slowly, Lucy and Jack emerged from the house. With each step, Lucy checked her footing. When she reached the sidewalk, she saw Tony, his arms stretched down under the pressure of two heavy cardboard boxes.

"Did the cable guy show up?" Tony said.

"Who?" Lucy bent at her knees, following Jack's lead, and placed the mirror on the ground. Gently, they leaned it against the front of the house, their hands cushioning it as it made contact with the wall.

"I ordered cable. We need cable, Luce." Tony put the boxes on the step, wiped his forehead, and stuck a hand in his jeans pocket to retrieve his smokes. "What's he doing here?"

"We're painting the living room, " Lucy said.

"You didn't tell me he was going to be here." Tony lit a cigarette.

Mrs. Donato arrived at Lucy's side. "Do you have time to look at a few of these?"

"Well, we just got started," Lucy said, eyeing Tony's cigarette.

"What are you doing?" One of the Delvecchio sisters stuck her head out of the window to the left of Lucy's house. "Just what do you think you're doing?" She flung her arms out the window as if she were about to catch a falling infant.

The other Delvecchio sister came outside and sprang to the mirror with surprising swiftness. Her back against the mirror, she stretched her arms out and placed her palms against the glass. "What's going on?"

Lucy felt as if she'd defiled a grave.

"She loved that mirror." The one in the window said.

"I'm sorry," Lucy found herself saying.

"It is a beautiful mirror," Mrs. Donato said.

"Thank you," the old sisters said in unison.

"You're taking it out?" Mrs. Donato gently put her hand on top of the mirror and cast a sympathetic glance to the sister holding herself against it.

"Yes," Lucy said.

"Ladies, if we could all calm down for a second, I'm sure we can arrange for one of you to have it," Jack began, trying to make eye contact with each of the women as he spoke.

"It belonged to our sister."

"Exactly. So what I'm suggesting . . . ," Jack said, his hand still resting on the top of the mirror.

"This is none of your business," Tony said. "We can handle this."

"It belongs in her house," a sister said.

"I was just trying to help," Jack said to Tony.

"I thought you didn't care what I did with the house," Lucy said to Tony.

"I didn't know you'd be throwing this out." He pointed to the mirror, to his mother, with the two fingers holding his smoldering cigarette. "And you didn't mention him."

It was as if he knew Lucy had kissed Jack.

Then came Colleen's sardonic nasal laugh. She sauntered across the street wearing her signature cropped jeans and an oversized Wildwood T-shirt. "What have we here?" She remained standing a safe distance away on the other side of a parked car.

They were officially a crowd now, filling the few feet of narrow sidewalk, their voices rebounding between the houses on either side of the street. Lucy stared at the legs reflected in the mirror.

"I'm sure we could bring it back in," Mrs. Donato said to her son. "It wouldn't be that much of a problem, would it?"

"But . . . ," Lucy said.

"I can see you posing in front of it in your wedding gown. Beautiful. Just beautiful," Mrs. Donato said.

Anne came out of the house. "What's the problem?"

"Jack and I took the mirror down, and the Delvecchio sisters think we shouldn't have," Lucy explained.

Anne descended the steps. For the first time since her arrival, she was showered and dressed, looking lovely in a light cotton skirt and sandals. "That thing." She waved her hand at the mirror. "It's atrocious. Good call."

A cacophony of squawks and hoots issued from the seniors gathered. Tony approached Jack, brandishing his dwindling cigarette, his chest mere inches from Jack's, demanding to know who Jack thought he was. At the same time, Anne chose to inform the Delvecchio sisters that their sister was dead and no longer needed the mirror.

After calmly attempting to insert herself into the various dialogues, Lucy gave up. She pushed past them and climbed the steps, feeling like a scab crossing the picket line.

"Go away," Lucy shouted. "All of you just go away. This is my house."

Momentary quiet. Stunned faces stared at her before she slammed the door. The frame of the house shook.

Someone yelled, "The mirror!" Lucy heard feet scampering.

How had all these people come into her life?

Anne was the first to knock on the door, demanding to know what she had done to be locked out, and wanting her stuff. Next, Tony pounded on the door, declaring it was his home. The others continued their protests in the street.

As Lucy walked to the kitchen, their voices faded. She sat in her chair, she stood, she sat again. Part of her wanted to go out and do battle with each of them. Another part of her wanted to take the entire contents of the house, piece by piece, and toss it out the window. Letting things land where they may. On whomever.

The bagels at the mouth of the brown paper bag made her think of the taste of Jack's kiss. She tossed the strays back in the bag and rolled the top of it down. She lit a cigarette and inhaled deeply. She loved Tony because he wanted her. And he was, in her estimation, worth loving. But with Jack, with Jack she wanted him. Particularly after their kiss. A long stream of smoke came from her mouth. She watched it slowly slither in the air above her as it moved toward the window. She produced another stream and imagined herself purging these men, these women, these things. Emptying herself of their needs, their wants, their noise.

Her mother's recipe box was now shrouded in a cloud of smoke. This was the place to start, Lucy decided. Randomly, she plucked cards from the box and set them aflame. As they burned, she placed their thumb-sized smoldering corners in the ashtray, and wished she'd bought a bigger house farther away. One with a fireplace.

A recurring nightmare, and sometimes daydream, surfaced in Lucy's mind. It took place on the night of her mother's death. In it, Lucy was the one in control, filled with rage and truly murdering her mother. Taking that pillow up in anger and holding it over her mother, who fought with every last bit of mortal energy to preserve her life. These thoughts invigorated her, made her feel powerful. But then she was always frightened. Frightened of what was inside her. Frightened of what Marge had unleashed in her.

The smoke alarm went off in the dining room, jarring Lucy. She climbed onto a chair, tossed the lid on the floor, and yanked the battery out. Then she remembered her jewelry box.

The twangy "Somewhere over the Rainbow" emanated from the box as she laid the papers in a row before her on the bed. What had Marge said that last night? Watching the doctor — watching Anne's father — on the news? Lucy could think of nothing but her task for that night. The pile of carefully written index cards. In the past when they followed this news story, she'd always been self-conscious, assuming that Marge's curiosity in this boy's fate was her way of making Lucy uncomfortable, subtly suggesting that Lucy wasn't far from being in the South American boy's predicament. That Marge had been watching the doctor had never occurred to Lucy.

"He is the same," Marge had said. Lucy had thought she'd meant the boy. "He is the same."

Marge wasn't the same. At the age of eighteen, she transformed herself into a middle-aged housewife. She had convinced herself that he was her one great love. He was her missed opportunity, her missed life. She tortured herself with this belief in order to justify the act of Anne's conception. It was not merely a moment of teenage passion, misguided emotions, or raging hormones. It was true love. In the end, unrequited love. A love that made her so weak she gave herself to a boy who didn't love her, who didn't want their child. She would never allow love to make her weak again.

"He is the same."

As he was then? As he was the last time she saw him? On television? In person? He was unaffected. Successful. He'd gotten from life what he'd expected. What had Marge's plans been? She never talked about her dreams or the future. She never talked about the past. She talked tasks. For decades Marge condemned herself to a passionless life. When cancer came, she welcomed it as if it were her long-lost lover finally come to take her away. But in the end, she grew impatient even with it.

"He is the same."

Lucy looked down to the pile that was her mother's obituary. "A Life of Giving." Had her last public statement been for his benefit? Did she believe or hope that he would read it, that he'd been watching for her too? Poor Marge. Suffering in silence, not being able to tell anyone of her pain so they could truly understand how strong, how stoic, she was. It must have been maddening.

Her mother had died on October 30, and Lucy wondered if this date was significant. Was it his birthday? The day they met? The day she gave herself to him? Or was it coincidence that he was going to be on the news that night? Again, Marge had left her with so much to sort through with no indicators of worth.

Lucy took it all — the holy card, the index cards, the cigarette box, the newspaper obituaries — into the bathroom. She sat on the toilet lid, wondering if her mother was watching, if she'd been watching all along. Memories of just the events that had happened in this tiled room in the past few months made Lucy nauseated.

But now Lucy knew. She knew her mother's biggest secret. Marge had been weak; she'd been frightened. Lucy's secret, too. Maybe that was what they shared. Lucy lit the first index card with her lighter, and then another card, then another. Marge's blue-ink-embossed cards twisted until the burnt remnants coated the sink like withered rose petals. Smoke filled the room.

*   *   *

Hours later, there was a light rapping on the screen door. At first, Lucy thought it might be the cable guy. But she found her sister waiting there with an inquiring expression on her face. Lucy opened the door. Anne looked up and down the street before entering.

"Your friend Colleen is insane," she said.

"I know, most people I know are," Lucy said, turning and walking to the kitchen. Everything was untouched. "I think it has something to do with her ex-husband."

"Is something burning?" Anne said quietly.

"Not now," Lucy said. The recipe box was still on the kitchen table. The burnt fragments lay in the ashtray. She dumped the ashtray and returned it to the table. She paused, then tossed the recipe box into the trashcan.

"Colleen cheated on him," Anne said, watching her sister's actions. "Did you know that?"

"She never told me," Lucy said.

"And he couldn't forgive her. That's why she's so angry, I guess." Anne dragged the side of her hand along the table top, collecting paper fragments. "That's what I have to do."

"What?" Lucy asked, seated now, letting her sister clean up after her.

"Forgive." Anne disposed of the fragments and ashes. She ran the water, waiting for it to get hot.

"Brad said he didn't actually . . . ," Lucy said.

"I know." With a moist sponge, Anne wiped the kitchen table, lifting the bagel bag to wipe away stray onion bits and sesame seeds. "But he was still wrong."

"What about Mom?"

"Let's not get crazy here. One thing at a time."

"All right," Lucy said.

There had always been tension between Marge and Anne. With Marge's after-death revelation, Lucy assumed it was because Anne reminded her mother, each and every day, that she had made a mistake. Marge had been like Anne before Eugene's rejection — passionate and excitable. So Anne was more than a physical reminder of Eugene's betrayal, she was a reminder of Marge's betrayal of herself. As Anne carried the dishes to the sink, Lucy watched her and hoped that her sister wouldn't resign herself to the same life Marge had lived.

"I'm sorry, Lucy."

"For what?"

"For being a pain in the ass. For taking it out on you."

"It's okay," Lucy said, and she meant it. As she sat watching her sister clean the coffee pot and mugs, Lucy realized that she still had a secret. The murder. Maybe she'd tell her sister someday. That also left at least one more secret Marge had.

"Sometimes I felt bad that I left you behind. And sometimes I thought you were the stronger one for staying," Anne said, finally sitting down next to Lucy. The kitchen was clean, everything in its place. "You're right that I need to figure it out with Brad. I was going to leave today, before you kicked me out."

"Sorry."

"Had my bags packed and everything. Then, slam!"

"I'm sorry."

"It's okay. It was great, actually. You should have seen the looks on their faces. Mine too, I guess. But how am I going to get my car out of that parking spot?"

"I'm going to call Jack in the morning. I can ask him."

Anne excused herself to take a shower, saying that she felt dirty after being in Colleen's house. The smell of the burnt index cards still permeated the house, and Lucy wondered if Anne hadn't asked what she had been burning because she herself had conducted a similar ceremony in her past.

Lucy walked into the living room and took in its emptiness; she'd really begun something that morning. She thought of the dirt and clutter in Colleen's house, each messy pile an eruption of anger; she thought of how Marge kept her anger buried in sameness and orderliness. Each house was the manifestation of emotions — uncontrolled and controlled.

She liked the emptiness of this room and the possibilities it offered, the colors and textures that she would bring to it.

From outside she heard the sound of fireworks and remembered that the Independence Day celebrations began tonight. She opened the door. The Delvecchio sisters were at their posts, and for a moment Lucy considered retreating inside, but she didn't. She sat on her stoop and lit a cigarette. It was quiet except for the festive explosions at the river. The sisters said nothing, acting as though Lucy wasn't sitting between them, a few feet away. The mirror still leaned against the front wall and reflected the row of homes across the street. The light of the television flickered in Colleen's house, and Lucy wondered if she was watching the fireworks on TV. The old women slowly retreated into their houses, first the one on the right, then the other, who murmured, "Some people's children," as her screen door slammed shut. Alone, Lucy finished her cigarette and flicked it into the gutter. The embers sputtered like fireworks.

Acknowledgments

To Anne Hood for selecting my book as the fiction winner of the 2007 Many Voices Project. To Alan Davis, Donna Carlson, and the team at New Rivers Press for creating a beautiful book.

Warm thanks to my first readers — Sarah Barr who encouraged and challenged me as I learned to be a writer and a mother, and Laura Jean Carney who always gave me a glass of wine before giving me her feedback. Thanks to the Bennington Writing Seminars, especially to Alice Mattison who was a strong advocate for Lucy from the first time she met her. This book would not exist without Alice. Also, to Mary-Beth Hughes and Elizabeth Cox for helping to shape the final draft, and to Askold Melnyczuk for making me take a break. To the nurturing and insightful Erin Hennicke, who'd make a fabulous literary agent, for introducing Lucy to the outside world. To Janet Benton and her writers' group for reading the first chapter a thousand times until I got it right. To my sister, Mary Barr Mann, who would put this book in the hand of every American, and then some. To my parents Tom and Mary, my first teachers, who gave me my love of books. To Oldrich and Vera Toman for all their support and babysitting. To my brother Tom, sister Jen, and all my friends who asked to read the book even before it found a home. To Frank Sinatra for keeping me company, sometimes in the "Wee Small Hours."

I have much love and gratitude for my husband Peter who gives me the foundation from which I can reach for my dreams. Thank you to my children for giving me discipline by teaching me to write in the time they gave me. Such good nappers they were.

Part of Chapter 1 appeared in *Philadelphia Stories*, Summer 2009, and part of Chapter 13 appeared as an excerpt from "The Late News" in the *Bennington Review*, January 2005.

Biography

Susan Barr-Toman was born and raised in Philadelphia, where she still lives with her husband and two children, and where she teaches writing at Temple University. She holds an MFA in writing and literature from the Bennington Writing Seminars. Visit her at www.susanbarrtoman.com.